C0-AOA-953

LOVE'S
DEATH

LOVE'S DEATH

OSCAR VAN DEN BOOGAARD

Translated from the Dutch by Ina Rilke

Farrar, Straus and Giroux
New York

PT
5881.12
.O56
L5413
2001

Farrar, Straus and Giroux
19 Union Square West, New York 10003

Copyright © 1999 by Oscar van den Boogaard
Translation copyright © 2001 by Ina Rilke
All rights reserved
Distributed in Canada by Douglas & McIntyre Ltd.
Printed in the United States of America
Originally published in 1999 by Em. Querido's
Uitgeverij BV, the Netherlands, as *Liefdesdood*
Published in the United States
by Farrar, Straus and Giroux
First American edition, 2001

Library of Congress Cataloging-in-Publication Data
Boogaard, Oscar van den.
    [Liefdesdood. English]
    Love's death / Oscar van den Boogaard ; translated by
Ina Rilke.– 1st ed.
        p.   cm.
    ISBN 0-374-18585-9 (alk. paper)
    I. Rilke, Ina.   II. Title.

PT5881.12.O56 L5413 2001
839.3'1364–dc21

                                                    00-047665

Special thanks to the Foundation for the Production and
Translation of Dutch Literature for a translation grant.

Designed by Holly McNeely

45044176

PART I

August 10, 1973

ONE

*T*here was once a sailor who swallowed the end of a rope and was hoisted up into the mast by his coiled entrails.

Eight-year-old girls don't understand such things.

Besides, all the way to the top . . .

Inez reclines on a deck chair, staring into the pool. The water heaves, laps against the sides. She counts. Eleven, twelve, thirteen.

Vera shoots up to the surface, waves her arms, paddles to the side, climbs onto the edge.

"Twenty-five."

"No, Inez, twenty-six. No cheating now!"

The little girl straightens her back, spreads her arms, bends her knees, leaps off the side into the light, draws up her legs, wraps her hands around her knees, plummets into the water.

Inez counts. Eleven, twelve, thirteen, fourteen.

The child shoots up, raises herself above the surface, waves her arms, paddles to the side, clambers onto the edge.

"Twenty-seven."

She straightens her back, spreads her arms, bends her knees, and leaps, draws up her legs, wraps her hands around her knees, and plummets into the water.

Inez counts.

She shoots up, raises herself above the surface, her long hair whips a spray of droplets across the buddleia, the honeysuckle, the garden statue. She paddles to the side, clambers onto the edge. "Inez?" she calls, breathlessly.

"Twenty-eight."

Inez screws up her eyes. The water doesn't get a chance to come to rest. Foreground dissolves into background. She gets up from her chair and walks to the house. In the windows she can see Vera's reflection as she leaps up. She shrieks like a bird. Inez opens the sliding glass doors and steps into the cool interior. The blackbird, she thinks. Last summer's blackbird never came back.

Inez pours a glass of lemonade in the kitchen and wanders outside again.

"Vera, come here!"

She has just vanished under the surface, the water

splashes on the tiles. She shoots up again, swinging her arms and her head.

"Vera, sweetie!"

The child races to the side, leaps up, and plummets into the water.

Too bad about the lemonade.

She leaves the glass on the poolside table and goes back inside. She seats herself in a leather armchair with her back to the window, presses her fingers to her temples. She can sit still in the same position for hours. People who spend a lot of time alone tend to become withdrawn. They end up not needing anyone at all. That's not what she wants. She would rather be with Hans. She follows him in her thoughts. He's lying in bed in his Boston hotel room. She snuggles up to him and lays her hand on his stomach. She always thought she would want children someday. A shrill cry in the distance. A frightened bird. Then all is silent. A schoolyard. A shower of rain. Dappled shade. A swimming pool. Clouds hanging low over the changing rooms. Inez opens her eyes. She gets up and steps outside.

"Vera! Vera?"

She tries to piece it all together later. The little feet reaching for the bottom so as to get a good thrust upward, kicking, still kicking. Before the body can rise up to the light of the world, the treetops, the month of August, the summer holiday, the days to come, the surprises, the things you will not be spared, the things you have to deal with so as to put them behind you—before then her last breath will have preceded her in a thousand tiny bubbles . . . perhaps inhaled by a bird, a squirrel, or a stick insect.

Come on, Inez thinks, up you come.

The child is lying on the bottom.

Don't play jokes on me!

The hair ripples like seaweed.

Come on, little girl, enough is enough!

Inez jumps fully clothed into the pool, ducks underwater to grab Vera. The child is heavy and slack. Inez raises her head above the surface, takes a gulp of air, and ducks again. She hooks her wrists under the child's armpits and pushes her feet against the bottom for leverage. The water comes up to Inez's chin. Summoning all her strength she hauls the child to the side. The face has turned blue, the brown eyes are wide open. Inez tries to lift her onto the side of the pool but her arms aren't strong enough. She sinks underwater, thrusts her head between Vera's legs, and hoists her up on her shoulders. She heaves her upward and tips her over the edge. She climbs out of the pool and crouches over Vera. The little body is covered in scratches and grazes, the skin is bluish gray, the pupils in the staring eyes are dilated. "Look at me," Inez screams, "it's me, look at me," but the eyes are dull. She pinches the arms and smacks the cheeks. Vera does not react. Her lips and nails are blue. Inez stares at the small chest, it's quite still; she puts her cheek against the nose and mouth, she can feel no air; she lays her index finger on the neck artery and gropes the wrist for the pulse, but there is no life; she lays her ear on the breast, but all she can hear is the pounding of her own heart. Holding the back of the neck with one hand and raising the chin with the other, she takes a deep breath, presses her mouth firmly on Vera's lips, and blows into her lungs. And again she takes a deep breath and blows into the little body. And again and again. Until she has no breath left. Her tears pour over Vera. She shakes the child, slaps the cheeks. "Please move, please," she sobs, "for my sake!" She takes the child's ankles and holds her upside down to let the water run out. She shakes her again, violently, but the body has stopped. She lays her on her back on the tile surround and runs into the house. She sinks onto a wicker chair and fastens her eyes on the bushes and the trees.

The summer child turns up with a striped towel around her neck. Holding a plastic bag. She drops towel and bag onto the deck chair, kicks off her sandals, unzips the front of her orange terry-cloth dress and lets it slide down. In her little blue swimsuit she skips over to the water, and then: splash! Vera puts her hands on the edge of the pool and her face breaks into a smile. She climbs out of the water, runs to the poolside table, and raises the glass of lemonade to her lips. She drinks it down in a few gulps and asks for a refill, and a sandwich please.

Inez opens her eyes. The water is perfectly still.

She tries again. Vera putting her hands on the edge of the pool and her face breaking into a smile. The dullness of the eyes. The trees fanning out and coming to a standstill. The sun standing still, nature standing still, the shadows all gone.

She is prepared for her own death but not for anyone else's. Time for action. What does she know about children? She bends down, tries to take Vera in her arms the way you scoop up a baby. She can't get the child off the ground. She has a bad back. Maybe take hold of the wrists and drag. And there's the wheelbarrow. No, she must carry Vera herself. Making a huge effort, she heaves the body over her right shoulder, clenches her arms under the buttocks, and carries her down the same path Vera came up this morning in her little terry-cloth dress. The little dress! She lays the child on the ground and goes back to the terrace, picks up the dress, warm from the sun, takes a quick look in the plastic bag: shampoo, box of crayons, sketch pad, plastic hairbrush. Inez takes the brush and heads back to Vera, her pace unhurried, for she must do all these things as correctly as possible. She opens the dress flat on the ground, lays Vera on top, pulls the arms through the sleeves, zips up the front, raises Vera's head, rests it on her knee, starts brushing the dark hair. "Come along, little girl," she says, "I'm going to take you home." Myriad flecks of light dance on the pale skin, she buries a kiss in the neck, takes the thumb into her mouth, mumbles "Goodbye, sweet, sweet Vera," and "We've got all the time in the world." She takes her in her arms again and tries to lift her up, but she's slippery and slides to the ground, limp, defeated. Inez presses the child to her chest, bears her along the borders with the red poppies, the white foxgloves, the yellow nasturtiums, the purple-plumed buddleia, the pale marigolds, under the pendulous wisteria blossoms, past the white roses blushed with pink on whippy branches shooting up from the shade to the sun, the velvety lamb's ears, the fleshy sea kale. Inez pauses in a clearing among the trees and bushes. This is where Hans burns brushwood and dead leaves. She sits down on the chopping block. In her arms Vera Klein, head lolling back, arms dangling, legs dangling–drowned, in Inez's swimming pool. The sailor surrenders to the inexorable mechanism of rope and entrails. A dumb animal with no will of his own. It's a matter of ABC. Inez must go the whole way to Calvary, following all the stations of the cross.

She carries Vera past the hydrangeas, the linden tree, the ferns, the rhododendrons, the oak tree, the birches with their carpet of moss, weeds, clumps of grass, pebbles, a tiny bird skeleton, soil, scraps of paper, a hairpin, past the beech hedge to the hole in the wire fence; she lays Vera down, crawls through the hole, and turns to pull Vera after her by the wrists. One, two. She glances over her shoulder. Through the bushes she can make out the family home with the lowered blinds. She drags the child through the flower bed and across the lawn, lets go of her by the croquet hoops and balls. She fingers the hair, smoothing it, cups her hands around the sallow face. She stands up, walks to the house, opens the screen door, and steps into the spotless kitchen with the gleaming sink. No sign of life. Inez calls "Oda! Oda!" but Oda has gone out for the day. Crossing the living room to the hall she calls Oda's name again. She enters the mother's study. On the desk a photograph of Vera. An only child. A sweet smile. Eyes narrowed to slits. The brown hair scraped into a little bun like a ballerina's. On the phone a sticker with the emergency number. She tries to breathe normally.

Inez walks down the driveway to the road. She waits by the border stones. The sun blazing on the asphalt, the poplar trees motionless in the silence. In the distance the stirrings of a tone. Several tones, becoming louder in spurts. The siren rips the silence to shreds. A rush of frenzy. Inez runs back to the house alongside the ambulance. The doors fly open. A man wearing a green cap jumps out, followed by two others in green and white, carrying bags and medical equipment. Inez leads them through the hall and kitchen.

"When did it happen?" someone behind her asks.

"Ten minutes ago, half an hour, an hour," she blurts breathlessly, pushing the screen door open.

The men charge across the lawn to the figure lying on the grass. They kick the Skippy ball and the croquet balls out of the way. One of them unzips the little dress and slits open the swimsuit. Another feels the neck artery, listens to the heart, studies the pupils. A small mask is placed over her nose and mouth, a saline drip inserted into her arm. Inez hears another siren approaching, she runs into the house, opens the front door, a huge ambulance is parked next to the station wagon, two men in white coats get out. Inez leads them quickly to the others. The men crouch over Vera. The IV drip and oxygen bottle are held up. She can hear the men counting out loud. Yet another siren. Inez races through the house to the front door. Two policemen get out of their car, ask her what the problem is. Inez tells them her neighbor's daughter has drowned in her pool. She leads the way.

"I can't see any pool," one of them says in surprise.

"In my garden," says Inez. "I live next door."

"So what's she doing here?"

"I took her home first."

Inez waits on the garden bench by the kitchen window. There are now five men huddled around Vera. She can hear a voice counting out loud and the deep intake of breath. The policemen crane their necks to follow what is going on. The man with the green cap takes two metal disks, rubs them together, and places them on Vera's chest, at which all five men rear up as a shudder passes through Vera's body. She bounces up, her head, arms, feet twitch, then she goes limp again, the men bend over her, feel her heart, her pulse, shake their heads, repeat the procedure, rear up as the little girl's body bounces up again, bend over her, feel her heart and pulse. The man with the green cap stands up, detaches himself from the huddle, and walks toward Inez with his eyes on the ground. The others pack away their instruments. The figure on the grass is a doll.

Everything turns blue before her eyes. Blue-black. Black. She can hear voices, not words, pounding in her head, her thoughts come to a halt at the Skippy ball, then drift on to the violets, the grass, the hairy arm, the shiny box, the gray sack, the doll zipped up in the sack, the sack being put in the box, the sun exploding on the closed lid, the black-coated backs, the bowed heads, past the roses, the tomatoes, the grapevine, the stack of logs, into the black van, rear doors shut, down the drive, gone.

Everyone's gone. Inez lays her head on the garden table. She tries to picture Vera the way she saw her the first time. Like a stray cat among the bushes. First they motion her to go away. But she doesn't budge. Such a pretty little thing. Then they coax her the way you coax a kitten. Hans clucks his tongue. Vera tiptoes to the edge of the pool and dips a finger in the water. They get up from their deck chairs, stoop, and hold out their hands to her. Vera runs off, but she comes back the next day. And the day after. Each time she comes nearer. One day she steps gingerly into the house. Hans shuts the sliding door behind her. The child is in the house. Inez imagines it is their own daughter who is wandering about in their art collection, looking at the paintings and sculptures.

Inez pauses at the foot of the wooden staircase in the hall. She glances outside. No one in sight. She goes upstairs. She's been there before. On the right the main bedroom. The door is open. The bed with the flowered bedcover. The snowy-white net curtains. The wooden crucifix on the green wall over the bed. The bedside lamps. The dressing table neat and tidy. The faint smell of hairspray and nail polish.

Across the stairs is the green bathroom. On the side of the bath a yellow plastic duck. On the washbasin a gaily colored tube of toothpaste. Through the red venetian blinds slices of trees, flagpole, and sky.

To the left of the stairs is the child's bedroom. Red carpet, little red desk, red chair. Bedcover and curtains patterned with red, blue, and green figures holding hands. A Cape violet growing in a purple plastic container on the windowsill. The door to the balcony is open. The pots with bamboo and papyrus, beyond them the trees and glimpses of thatch roof. She turns the knob of the closet door and opens it. Neatly stacked clothes folded by a motherly hand and bare shelves with sachets of lavender.

On the little red desk lies a drawing. It is inscribed with red curly letters:

To Emil from Vera

The drawing is of a sort of bubble. The world outside the bubble is divided in two. The top half is blue sky, the bottom is green ground. Inside the bubble a tree. A grinning yellow sun with a lion's mane. A big brown bird. A girl with a scooter. An empty house. The door is open. Has the bird escaped? The girl and the bird are heading in opposite directions. The girl is going home. She is alone. Shut in by the blue and the green of the world. The girl and the bird in the bubble. And the house.

TWO

Around the corner of the shed the father swerves into view riding his bicycle. He is wearing his green military uniform. His beret. Whistling "Oh When the Saints." He stops by the rambler rose, swings his leg backward over the saddle, and dismounts. He says, "What a surprise."

Inez gets up from the garden bench, her lips trembling.

"What's wrong, Inez?"

She has rehearsed her reply. "What I'm going to say is very difficult."

Paul's expression darkens. His fingers grip the handlebars.

Her voice falters. She can't do it.

"Go on, tell me."

Inez draws herself up and looks into his pale eyes. "Vera has drowned." Her voice sounds calm and detached. "They've taken her to St. Anthony's."

His face crumples up as he swerves away from her. He wheels his bicycle into the shed. She can hear the click of the kickstand. "Where's Oda?" he calls out from the shadowy interior.

"I don't know. She sent Vera to me this morning."

There is no sound from the shed. Inez is at a loss. She goes into the shed and puts her arms around the man standing next to the bicycle. His arms hang stiffly by his sides. She can feel the rough fabric of his uniform, the cold buttons. He moves out of her embrace, walks outside, and stands still in the orange glow under the awning. His hand at his throat. "How did it happen?"

"I don't know."

"Was she alone?"

"I was in the house."

"Did she fall? Did she bump into something?"

"She was lying on the bottom of the pool. I got her out and called an ambulance. They tried to resuscitate her." Inez sits down on the garden bench. "I did all I could."

"Where can Oda be?" Paul asks wretchedly.

"She didn't say where she was going. She just phoned to ask if it was all right for Vera to stay with me until you got home."

"I'm going to change my clothes," Paul says, entering the house. He shuts the screen door behind him. The refrigerator switches off with a shudder. Inez pictures Paul shedding his uniform, becoming a man who can weep.

Losing one's parents is tragic, losing one's lover unbearable, losing one's child worst of all. The hierarchy of grief. Oda could arrive any minute now. What can she say to her? What does she know about parenthood? If only she could go home, lock the doors, draw the curtains, crawl into bed, fall asleep. She is dead tired, can't stop her head from dropping onto her chest.

Footsteps in the house. The screen door swings open. Paul, wearing jeans and a blue polo shirt, comes to her side. "Can you stay here until Oda gets back?"

"Of course," Inez replies. "I'll stay."

Paul heads across the lawn toward the flagpole. He stops by the hedge and stares down the road. He stands there for ten minutes, twenty minutes, half an hour. Inez goes after him, positions herself behind him, a little to the side. "Do you want to go and see Vera now?" she asks carefully.

"I'm not going without Oda," he says resolutely. "She must have gone shopping. The shops close at six."

Two teenage girls with wet hair ride past on their bicycles, holding hands, giggling. A whiff of chlorine. Paul walks to the section of lawn set aside for the rabbits. He crouches down and sticks a finger through the wire netting. He wanders back to the house, raises the lid of the rain barrel, and dips his hand in the water, then goes into the shed, opens the partition to the garage. He opens the garage door, walks down the drive, and waits by the border stones. The cairn of the dead, Oda would say.

Inez sits at the kitchen table. She watches as Paul retrieves the Skippy ball from the bed of violets and carries it into the shed with both hands. He pulls the croquet hoops out of the grass, gathers up the balls and mallets, and deposits them in their cart, which he rolls into the shed. He fills the metal watering can in the rain barrel and disappears around the corner. A moment later he returns, puts the watering can down next to the barrel, comes into the kitchen, and seats himself beside her.

"They should have left her here," Inez whispers. "You could have been with her all this time."

Paul pushes his chair back and gets up. He goes to the study. Inez hears him lifting the receiver and dialing a number, replacing the receiver, lifting it again, and dialing anew. A click. Then silence. Inez follows him into the study. She rests her hand on his shoulder. Paul turns slowly, looks up at her. "Everyone's out," he says, adding, "Don't you want to get changed? You're all dirty."

She looks down. Her white trousers and pale blue blouse are smeared with mud. Her sandals filthy. Her arms covered in scratches. Her nails rimmed with black.

Inez shuts the front door behind her and decides to take the long route home, via the driveway. Fearful of meeting Oda, she breaks into a run. First she must talk to

Hans. She jumps over the uneven flagstones that are be-ing pushed up by the roots of the ash tree. The sun hangs low over the trees at the end of the road. What time could it be? Her pace slackens once she is past her mailbox. She walks up to the house, panting. The water in the pool is perfectly still. The sliding doors are open. Inez sits down on the sofa and dials the number on the note by the phone.

"I've been trying to reach you for hours," Hans says irritably.

"Why, what's the matter?"

"I've got another of those ulcers under my tongue. It hurts when I talk. Do I sound strange at all?"

"Hans . . ."

"How on earth can I give my speech tonight? I mean, people will think there's something wrong with me. I can't understand how this can have happened. I make sure my vitamin intake is okay, and I always try to get enough sleep, you know that."

Inez has to interrupt him. "Vera drowned in our pool today."

It is deathly quiet at the other end. Inez presses the receiver into her lap. She stares at the gray monochrome on the wall over the dining table. She can't think and she can't feel. When she lifts the receiver to her ear the line is dead.

THREE

*I*nez freezes at the border stones, her heart thumping in her throat. Oda's metallic yellow car is pulling up in front of the garage. It's a matter of seconds now. Paul comes out of the house and runs to the car. Oda gets out, unsuspecting, sunglasses in her hair. Paul puts his mouth to her ear and clasps her hands. Inez lowers her eyes. Wild strawberries. A strangled groan. Silence. Death. Inez lifts her eyes cautiously. Paul and Oda have gone. She walks slowly to the house. The front door is open. They are standing in the hallway. Paul in his wife's arms. Oda stares blankly at Inez. "My child is dead," she says in a voice from another planet, uttering the words separately as if they were unconnected and devoid of sense and purpose. "Are you coming with us?"

. . .

Paul is at the wheel. Oda holds the rear door open. Inez gets in and slides to the middle of the backseat. The car rolls down the driveway and turns into the road at the border stones. Oda lights a cigarette. Inez can tell that the two figures in front of her are staring straight ahead. Paul's hand rests on Oda's knee. Inez avoids looking in the rearview mirror. She's afraid of meeting Paul's eyes. The car fills up with cigarette smoke. The window on her right is covered with stickers of horses, dogs, dolls.

They pull into the hospital parking lot, which is deserted except for a few cars. It is past visiting time. The weekend has begun. Inez trails after Oda and Paul. An arrow says MORTUARY. Stone paths lead past flower-filled borders. Paul holds the double doors open for Oda and Inez. The man at the counter directs them to the end of the corridor. The card in the plastic holder on the door has "Vera Klein" written on it. Oda and Paul go in. Inez waits on a bench in the corridor. She pulls a tissue from the box on the table next to her and blows her nose. Right now Hans will be telling his colleagues about the death of the little girl next door. He is blameless, and that is what makes the difference between him and her. Inez waits half an hour, an hour. Past the door at the end of the gleaming corridor she can see the slow fading of the day.

It is half past ten. Vera's door flies open. Oda stumbles into the corridor. Paul follows his wife at a slower pace. When the double doors swing to behind them, Inez gets up and slips into Vera's room. The child is lying under a white, floor-length sheet. She looks suspended in air. The head resting on a lace pillow. The sheet drawn up under the chin. The hair combed back, the eyes closed, the pinched lips painted pale pink, a grim cast to her features. *Vera in ire.* Sometimes Inez would find her asleep in their bedroom. The child would sneak into their house to take a nap. As if that were not possible in her own home.

"Oda's vanished," a voice behind her says. Paul is at the door, out of breath. "Are you coming?"

Inez follows him down the long corridor outside. Oda's car is the only one left in the parking lot.

"What do you want me to do?" Inez asks.

"Stay here until I find her." Paul hurries back to the reception area. Inez waits by the car, scanning the surroundings. She spots some kids on roller skates in the distance, near a lamppost. There is no one else in sight. Where would you find someone overwhelmed by grief?

    Leaning against a shed in a back garden

    On someone's doorstep

    In a squalid snack bar with her back to the door

    In a heavily shaded park

    In a church pew all the way at the back

    With a girlfriend.

Oda doesn't have any girlfriends in this town. They all live far away. They keep in touch by phone.

Paul returns without Oda. "No one's seen her," he says despondently.

Inez tries to reassure him. "She must have gone home, surely."

"Let's go."

They get into the car. While they are driving they keep trying to catch sight of Oda. They think they glimpse her riding a bicycle, in a car, at the checkout counter in a gas station, but each time they slow down to get a closer look, it turns out to be someone else. They drive through the leafy suburb with the ornamental ponds reflecting the lights in the villas.

"Oda used to like going for walks here with Vera," Paul says, as if they have both been erased from the here and now.

The house is shrouded in darkness. Paul asks Inez to wait there for Oda to return. She brushes his cheek with her fingers and gets out of the car. Paul opens the front door to let her in and drives off. Inez stands in the dark hallway. She calls out "Oda," just as she did this afternoon. No response. Inez turns on the lights. She is scared. Oda is not in the study, not in the living room, not in the kitchen. Inez goes upstairs, opens doors, turns lights on, climbs the stairs to the attic, can't find the light switch. The headlights of a car sliding along the rafters make her jump, her eyes fill with tears. She stumbles down both flights of stairs and slumps onto the living room sofa.

Inez thinks back to how she met Oda. First there was her voice. Low-pitched, seductive, firm. Her face over the hedge. A good-looking woman. Statuesque. Vera looks like her. Brown eyes. Narrow face. Dimples. How old would she be? Forty, maybe. "Would you care to come for a drink sometime?" Inez asks politely.

She does come over one evening, bringing Paul and Vera. The little girl leads her mother to the monochrome over the dining table. Mother and daughter facing the gray canvas. Oda says she thinks it's amazing. Hans shows Paul the photograph of the man with the mirror eyes. They go off together. Oda takes a seat next to Inez on the sofa. She lights a cigarette and says she teaches German, substituting for teachers who are sick or on maternity leave. It's nice not being tied down to a particular school, as she gets tired of seeing the same faces all the time. She glances at Vera twisting around on the swivel chair. "I want to spend a lot of time with her," she says with a smile.

The visit is reciprocated a few weeks later. A living room furnished with antiques. Logs burning in the grate. A little tray with packs of cigarettes on the coffee table. A silver lighter. Flowers in a vase. An ornamental candle the same color as the flowers. In the cabinet a sort of official portrait. Oda in a long gown, satin gloves going up past her elbows, Paul in white evening dress looking at her in admiration.

Oda is an attractive woman. She has good legs. She issues Paul instructions with her chin. He puts a log on the fire and opens a bottle of wine.

Inez can feel a headache coming on because of the

stuffiness, the nicotine fumes, the heat of the fire. She asks for an aspirin. Oda takes her upstairs and gives her a tablet and a glass of water. While they are seated on the bed side by side Oda studies Inez's nails. She says she should try using nail hardener. Inez looks at the dressing table. Jars and tubes in neat rows. A golden can of hairspray. Inez feels like a boy in this woman's presence. She notices flower-print curtains, a large crucifix above the bed, a portrait of the Queen and Prince Consort. Behind one of the doors on the landing Vera is asleep in bed.

The tone of the friendship has been set. Oda has claimed the right to fuss over Inez. Now and then she brings her little bunches of flowers. Posies, Oda calls them. Inez doesn't like flowers in the house, so she puts them in the garage. Quite often Oda asks Inez if it's all right for Vera to spend the afternoon at her house. She rolls up in her car, drops Vera at the front door, and drives off. To one of her schools? To town to buy clothes? To the hairdresser? Where on earth does Oda go?

FOUR

*I*nez has dozed off on the sofa. She wakes with a start, catches sight of her reflection in the window. She gets up and draws the curtains. It is just after two o'clock. There is a window banging upstairs. She crosses to the hall. The front door is shut. Stepping into the study she is overcome with dizziness. She holds on to the doorknob and the edge of the desk to steady herself. "I know you're there," she says timidly. The sound of a car pulling up. A door slamming. Footsteps on the flagstones. A key turning in the lock. She looks around apprehensively. In the hall mirror she sees Paul shutting the door behind him.

"Not here yet?" he asks.

"No."

"No phone call?"

"No."

Inez sinks onto the chair by the desk. Paul comes to her side. "I've looked for her everywhere," he says. Laying his hand on her shoulder he gazes at the photograph of his daughter. Oda's diary is open at today's entry. There's a little cross in the middle of the blank page.

"Did you talk to the police?" Inez asks.

"I'm going to wait until it's light."

"Poor Oda."

"She'll be here any minute now."

"Of course."

"I'll run a bath for her and pour her a glass of wine."

"She'll be exhausted."

"I'm glad you're here," Paul says. "Where is Hans, by the way?"

"He's in the States. He'll be back for the funeral."

"Funeral," mumbles Paul, "or cremation." He turns around and goes upstairs.

Inez glances at the clock. Three o'clock. She peels the foil off the dish standing on the sink. Endive with ham and cheese, prepared by Oda. She switches the oven on and sets the table. She slides the dish into the oven and wonders whether she should put some candles on the table. Perhaps not. She goes upstairs. Paul is seated on Vera's bed. On his lap the drawing. Inez sits down beside him and lays an arm around his shoulders. "Is Emil a boy in her class?" she asks.

Paul takes her hands and kisses them. "Emil is my old friend."

Feeling his breath on her throat, she begins to tremble. She's bewildered by her own emotions. "Let's have some food," Inez suggests.

Paul and Inez sit at the table. Paul fidgets with his knife and fork. "Yesterday, no, the day before yesterday, it was our tenth wedding anniversary. I'd booked a table at our favorite restaurant. Oda didn't feel well and went to bed early. I thought, Okay, we'll make up for it this weekend. I called the restaurant and told them I wanted a table for three on Saturday, seven o'clock." He puts his knife and fork down next to his plate. "Today's Saturday."

"Try to eat something."

"I can't." Paul's eyes are fixed on the kitchen door. "I can't think of Vera because I keep thinking of Oda."

Inez eats the endive. She doesn't touch the ham. Paul stares in front of him. "If someone told you you'd have a child someday and that you'd lose it, what would you do?"

Inez looks silently at Paul.

"Well, what would you do?"

"I don't know, Paul."

"You're young and you're stationed in a tropical country. Your buddies are sitting around you in a circle, joking and laughing. A toothless old woman looks at you with glazed eyes, she's smoking opium, she belongs to the jungle, the wild animals . . . You think the army chaplain who's translating for you is pulling your leg, you forget what the old woman said, you get on with your life, with the war, but the day your wife tells you she's pregnant you turn out not to have forgotten at all. Still, you dismiss the memory lurking at the back of your mind because the life budding inside her is far more potent, you insist on forgetting and you keep trying to forget, and because you keep trying you keep being reminded. The memory's there when you hold your child in your arms, it wakes you up in the night. You push it away, but it bounces back like a punching bag." Paul clears his throat. "I keep seeing that glazed look, whereas I want to think of Vera's sparkling eyes . . ."

Inez takes Paul's hand in hers. His expression is inward-looking.

"With hindsight, the men's laughter has an evil edge to it, they're laughing at the grief that hangs over your head, and the one who laughs loudest is your best buddy because his laughter is your shield, it's all just a big joke, a killing joke. You want desperately to stand beside him and join in with his laughter."

Paul gets up and goes to the window. He stares outside. "Imagine if she doesn't come back," he says. "Then I won't have anyone left. No one at all."

It is dark outdoors and dark indoors. The clock spreads a soft glow. It is 3:55 a.m. The little cross in black ink floats across her mind's eye. The mast of the ship. The lonely sailor dangling from the top, staring over the ocean. Upstairs in the bathroom the grieving father and waiting husband is taking a shower. In a while it will be morning, the priest will come and the undertaker and the school principal and the family doctor, he will have to make decisions about cremation, burial, coffin, clothing, gravestone, the size of the fleet of cars, the wording of the death announcement, the service, the music. Paul will wait until Oda returns.

The sound of gushing water has been going on for over an hour. Inez climbs the stairs. The bathroom door is ajar, she calls Paul's name, there is no reply, she glances at the bedroom door, it is shut, she knocks, no reply, back to the bathroom. The monotonous rush of water scares her, he can't have . . . She calls his name again, pushes the door open carefully, the empty bath, the toilet, the washbasin, the unfogged mirror, his silhouette behind the shower doors. Inez calls out "Paul!" Still no reaction. She steps forward anxiously, slides the shower door open. There he is leaning against the wall, his arms held stiffly by his sides, his chin on his chest, his skin cold to the touch. She turns the taps off, leans back to pull a towel from the rack, steps into the shower stall, and starts drying him off. "Paul," she whispers, rubbing his back, his arms, his legs. She rubs harder. "Paul, please," she says, and slaps his face, grabs him by the shoulders, shakes him hard until his arms come to life. He raises his head, clings to her like a child, buries his face in her neck. She leads him out of the shower, makes him sit on the rim of the bathtub, stands in front of him, drapes the towel around his shoulders, rocks him in her arms. Shivering, teeth chattering, he presses his head against her body, locks his legs around her legs, digs his fingers into her lower back while she rubs the towel over his wet hair. She feels a tingle in the pit of her stomach. Then the sound of a car stopping in the road, a door being slammed, a car driving off. Inez breaks away from Paul and runs to the bedroom. She sweeps the curtain aside. In the bleak light of dawn she sees a small figure coming up the drive. A suitcase in each hand, "Oda's back!" Inez cries. She races down the stairs and flings the front door open. Oda is standing on the doorstep, flanked by two suitcases. Oda gives Inez the saddest smile she has ever seen.

PART 2

November 1980

ONE

*F*or the last time Paul steps onto the diving board at his
pool in Paramaribo, straightens his back, stretches
his arms along his body, fixes his eyes on the end of the
board, inhales deeply, takes three rapid steps, pushes off
the edge with his left foot, swings his arms, and dives,
head tucked between his shoulders. He slices the surface
with his fingertips and shoots away underwater to re-
appear a few yards on, planting each arm ahead in turn
and moving his legs swiftly up and down, following the
dark line on the bottom of the pool. Every three strokes
he takes a sideways gulp of oxygen and breathes out underwater; at the far end of the line he bends his upper
body, draws up his legs, rolls over, clings to the side,
pushes off, and follows the line back again to the other
end, weightless and ageless, the way he was when he

was seven, fourteen, twenty-five. He's still the same now, at fifty-six. He speeds up his strokes, imagines he's crossing the ocean, swimming back to Oda.

After the hundredth lap he rests his elbows on the edge of the pool. Bakabana walks heavily from the terrace toward the house. She's wearing her red dress for special occasions, gold earrings, and bangles. Jane's playing with her doll on the doorstep. Paul rises out of the water and climbs onto the side. The mother and daughter disappear into the house. He brushes the drops off his body with the flat of his hands and reaches for the towel waiting for him over the back of his chair. He takes a seat at the table and pours himself a glass of fruit juice. He eats a roll spread with jam, watching Bakabana's movements behind the bedroom window. She's packing his suitcases. Now and then she gives her daughter instructions. Paul rereads the letter that came this morning. It's from Hans and Inez. Their request has come too late. His departure was unforeseen. He can feel the eyes of his olive-green friend on him. The mythic creature with its crest and frilled spine shifts its gaze from Paul to Bakabana and back again, as though putting two and two together, as though realizing it will soon have to forgo Paul's presence.

COUNT YOUR BLESSINGS

ODA READS THE WORDS OUT LOUD. She leans forward over her desk in her study, in her house, draws on her cigarette, stares at the embroidered motto. She counts the paper clips (seventeen), the elastic bands (twelve), the drawing pins (twenty-three), the supermarket savings stamps (one hundred and three).

Try thinking of gray, Paul would advise her. Not dark gray, not pale gray either, just medium, boring, foggy gray, the kind of fog that makes you slow down on the road, keep a safe distance.

Her fingers riffle through the file with addresses. She draws out the first card in the A slot and puts it face up by the phone. Her fingers slide over the silver rabbit box her brother bought her years ago in Phnom Penh. A pillbox. Pills for sleeping, for relaxing, for forgetting. She has flushed the forget-me-not pills down the toilet. Let her memories be siphoned away, let them discharge into the ocean and be borne to a distant place, where they can, for all she cares, lead a life of their own

Stop!

among shoals of tropical fish, or become entangled with seaweed, or twisted into the propeller of an oil tanker, or else harden

Stop!

into blood-red coral or sink to a wreck on the seabed amid Chinese porcelain and gold ducats, never to be recovered

Gray! Think gray!

as the tiny frogman descending to the deep would think one day

.   .   .

37

that was close . . .

So long as they stay together she must be kind to the rabbit. Its left ear is stored in its stomach. Knocked off by her overzealous cleaning lady. And instead of telling her she had broken it, she had simply left the ear lying next to the rabbit. As if the ear had fallen off all by itself. Like an autumn leaf. Or as if there had been a strong draft. Or an extraordinary case of metal fatigue. My my, the ear must have thought, I can't keep this up. Or perhaps the cleaning lady had meant her to think she herself was to blame. What a crazy idea. Imagine breaking off that dear little rabbit's ear on purpose. A typical example of desk vandalism. You could snap a pencil in two, say. Wrench blotting paper out of the writing pad. Smash the paperweight to smithereens. Rip up the notebook. Wreck the letter scale with a single blow of your fist. Or you could give up on the study altogether–not that you did much studying anyway–and slam the door behind you once and for all.

PAUL TAKES A SHOWER, SHAVES BY the washbasin, and showers again. He clips his nails, cleans his ears, and gets dressed. Bakabana has laid out his clothes for the flight home: white shirt, white trousers, black tie, black shoes, regulation white jacket with bar and stars, white cap with black braid and gold laurel. Paul looks in the

38

mirror to pin on his medals and ribbons and steps outdoors with his cap under his arm. He greets the chauf-
feur carrying his bags to the Mercedes. Bakabana is
waiting for him with a sprig of scarlet jungle flame from
the garden and some fruit in a plastic bag. She asks if
they can come along to the airport, but Paul says he'd
rather go alone. She draws a breath between clenched
teeth to show her displeasure. Jane would so love to go.
The little girl beside her is wearing a pale yellow dress,
white patent leather shoes, and white socks. The hair in
pigtails tied with yellow ribbons. Dressed for an outing.
Paul picks her up and plants a kiss on her forehead. He
hands her over to Bakabana and heads toward the car.
Bakabana and Jane follow him to the gate. Hearing a
thud behind them they turn to see the iguana prowling
along the side of the pool, then vanishing behind the
house. Jane starts to cry. Paul raises his hand in farewell
to the mother and daughter and gets into the car. As they
drive off Paul stares ahead. Leave-taking is not his forte.

THE LIEUTENANT COLONEL HOLED UP in his tropical tight
spot, melting pot, fleshpot . . .

Stop!

Bakabana sways, Bakabana lists, Bakabana keels on
the bed next to the lieutenant colonel. Her dress comes
away like banana peel.

Gray!

O luscious Bakabana, he mutters, cook of cooks, all
that cooking, licking, looking . . .

Stop!

Cooking, licking, looking.

Bakabana has fed him for years, he's been her mouth to feed, and now he's about to return the compliment by feeding *her* mouth, spilling his coconut sap

Gray!

in her jungle, flooding her flora and fauna.

The thinking must stop. Now! He can gobble her up, or she him, for all she cares.

For all she cares he'll never come back. Her Bonnie lies over the ocean.

Too late now, the lieutenant colonel has put his tropical hotspot behind him, beneath him, where, from the sky, it looks just like—yes, that's it, like a vast cabbage patch. The lieutenant colonel is returning home after years of heroism overseas—what do you mean by home, this is no longer his home, time he got that into his head, staying abroad for years and years and then coming home all of a sudden because they don't need him anymore. The lieutenant colonel will take his suitcases upstairs into the bedroom, the room where he once stretched his limbs, where he once turned his back to her . . . and he's in for a surprise.

Oda picks up the Papermate, the pen with the little heart, *un coeur simple,* an animated pen with a tiny heart pumping the ink through its body. She bought it because the man in the stationery shop told her you can write with it horizontally, too. Which is handy if you do crossword puzzles in bed. Did he think that just because her husband is away . . . Why doesn't he concentrate on that wife of his behind the half-drawn curtain, no doubt doing the accounts? Wasn't she one of the mothers she used to see waiting by the school playground?

She needed a notepad. And a couple of birthday cards. The tulips maybe. Or the family on the globe. A boy lingering near the comic books was clearly stealing looks at the men's magazines. A nice-looking boy. A loner. You could tell. The kind of boy who has a vivid, terrifying imagination full of self-reproach. Oda has spent a lot of time watching other people's children.

And index cards. And I'll have that Papermate as well. The shopkeeper grins. He's good at selling his wares, especially to women, and there are plenty of women on their own in this respectable neighborhood. And some crosswords, please. There was a wide selection. She left the shop with three crossword magazines. The shopkeeper's wife emerged from behind the curtain and joined her husband in the doorway. Oda wished them a nice day. Just before driving off she stuck her hand out of the car window to wave at them.

At Fat Otto's she bought a box of matches for the fireplace. While she was paying for them she allowed herself to be persuaded to buy some floating candles. To light up her lonely hours, he must be thinking. She could see the flames flickering in his eager eyes. And a bar of red coconut soap for Paul. "It's been a long time since you bought that," Fat Otto said. It sounded patronizing.

Suddenly she noticed the same boy she had seen before. He stood facing the row of glass jars filled with licorice. He pointed out the different sorts he wanted Otto to put in his paper bag. Oda sat in her car and waited for the boy to come outside. She wanted to have another look at him. He was good-looking, finely built. A Little Lord Fauntleroy. Surely he ought to be in school at this hour. What was taking him so long? Could he be chatting with the fat creep? As she turned onto the road she saw him in her rearview mirror emerging from the shop and undoing the lock of his bicycle. Driving home she wondered, What will his mother find in his pockets before she drops his trousers in the washing machine?

A paper clip
A nail
An elastic band
An eraser
A walnut
A Smurf
A Lego brick
A shard from an antique vase.

Oda makes a note on her new pad with her new pen: Take rabbit to jeweler. She pushes up her sunglasses. Finishes her glass of whiskey. Fumbles in her handbag hanging from the back of the chair for a pack of cigarettes, stands up. She checks with her finger to see whether the plant in the brass pot in the alcove needs watering. It does. Don't put off until tomorrow what you can do today.

Clouds beneath the wings, thin air above, weightless dusk higher still, ghostly swathes of mist streaming past, strange beasts advancing across the banked clouds, a horse, a unicorn, the sun poised to set in the deep, clouds resembling tombstones, candy floss, poodles, elephants with raised trunks, long-eared hares with their eyes shut, a tunnel filled with a great roar, voices in the background, a playground, a campsite, the orange light of a tent, shadows of children on the canvas, his knee being brushed by the hand of a girl walking down the aisle. Things never vanish without a trace, things and people may get lost, but never completely, those supposedly forgotten memories hover around waiting to be borne aloft by a bird on the wing, or they go off on their own through the universe seeking a haven in someone else's dreams or fantasies, or else they just drift without aim in the weightless dark . . . nothing ever goes away altogether . . . When the red light goes on, we're ready for the sergeant to shout, "Number one." Then we all huddle up close together and we jump through the door, one by one . . . How did it go again, the "Red River Rock"? . . . When you're heading down for a landing, just remember your sergeant's advice, "Keep your feet and your knees close together, and you'll meet Mother Earth very nice. So now, boys, lift up your glasses steady, for a toast

43

to the men of the sky, or a toast to the men dead already, and three cheers for the next man to die."

THE FIRST THING HE WILL ASK HER is what she has been doing while he was away. She has done nothing. She has enjoyed being on her own. But she keeps this to herself. "Enjoyed" is not the right word, "savored" is more like it. His absence meant that the days and nights were hers to be structured as she pleased. First she wanted to explore the emptiness. To immerse herself in it while it was still untainted. She listened keenly to the absence of footfalls on the stairs, of doors being opened and shut, of a voice calling her name. The bed beside her was not slept in. His breathing no longer set the rhythm of the night. But the very first evening of longed-for quiet was rudely interrupted. The phone rang. Paul's voice came from a different world. He was upset because the line had been busy all the time. While he launched into a detailed account of his doings, Oda repeated over and over under her breath, I don't want this. She had no desire to know what he had been doing, whom he had run into, what he was thinking. She clenched her fists. The man alone in his hotel room made her sad. If she felt like talking to a friend on the phone she didn't want to be hampered by the thought of him in his lonely lair trying to reach her, despondently replacing the receiver. She didn't want to feel pity.

· · ·

PAUL HAS DOZED OFF ON THE PLANE. He dreams of a summer day. A steel-blue sky. He's in his car, with the sunroof open. He can drive as fast or as slow as he pleases, he can go in any direction he likes. There's no one waiting for him. On the riverbank he can see a little girl with a fishing net. He stops the car and rolls down the window. She doesn't seem to notice. He observes her in the landscape. Windmill, meadow, fringe of trees, water, girl. A static image, in which no one has the capacity to move but he. He leaves his car on the shoulder and walks toward her, treading carefully. He sits down next to her on the grass. Neither of them speak. The little girl scoops up a dead fish in her net, lays it on the bank. She takes a stick and starts poking the fish. She breaks the stick in two and gives him half. While they stab the fish in turn he notices a mass of details: the silver rims around the clouds, the bald patches in the grass, the tufts of horsehair on the barbed-wire fence. Then he asks her, "Where will you sleep tonight?" The little girl is silent. She is lost in thought. Because she does not reply he repeats his question: "Where will you sleep tonight?"

DOWNSTAIRS IN HER STUDY SHE REREADS Paul's last letter. There is a Dutch stamp on the envelope.

Dear Oda,

This will be my last letter from Paramaribo.
This morning I handed over the paperwork and

the keys to Hermans. Gierstra should be landing
right now at Zanderij. I took care of some bills
and discussed plans for the party this evening
with Bakabana. This time next week I'll be at
Zanderij myself, boarding the plane home.
Hooray! Just a few obstacles left to be dealt with,
a piece of cake.

Hooray! This is bizarre. Now he's been recalled, he's
suddenly looking forward to coming home. What's that
hurrah to her? Paul thinks anything is worth three
cheers, even obstacles. Paul likes obstacles, they give
him a brief sensation of being alive.

The barbecue tonight (approx. 70 guests) will be
fun, tomorrow evening there's a farewell cocktail
party in my honor at Berkhof's (approx. 50 guests,
including the ambassador), on Wednesday
Lodewijk is hosting a dinner (approx. 12), and on
Thursday there'll be drinks at the embassy.
Gierstra's duty-bound to get something organized
for me, too, but somehow I don't think he'll get
popular as it is. I'm turning into quite a party man!

Is that really what it says? Paul a fun-loving, popular,
party man?

The moving men are coming on Monday. I hope
the boxes will get there before your birthday,
because I have a present for you. You'll like it.
And we'll go and buy you a new dress for your
birthday, too. You can pick something really

46

special because my finances are looking quite good. These final days and hours are taking far too long. Johnny has started work on a white safari suit for you, which I will bring with me in the suitcase along with the altered khaki trousers plus belt. My dearest, what more could you want?

Mr. Party Man coming home with armfuls of presents! A safari suit, so convenient for her jungle expeditions in the garden, when she peeks through the beech hedge at the gardener next door and can't help noticing the slab of white flesh that is bared each time he stoops to pick something up or pull out a nettle, as off-putting as exposed gums, no, she'll try to look the other way and who knows, maybe she'll spot a little nest in the bushes crammed with baby birds shrieking for their mother, and those khaki slacks will be just great for looking the part of Mrs. Party Man, it's like what all those homeless people do, especially if they're old: stick to beige, faded blue, flesh-colored, so as to be as inconspicuous as possible. And then off to Fat Otto's together to stock up on creams that will prevent her from aging prematurely, after that to the creepy stationer's to get even more crossword-puzzle magazines, until they've done them all and there's not a single one left. Dearest oh dearest, what more could you want? That sounds like an old song. So does "Ladybird, Ladybird, fly away home, the house is on fire and your children all gone." There's more to nursery rhymes than meets the eye.

Sent off change-of-address cards. Stopped automatic payments. Left money with Hermans for belated phone bills. Have let my hair grow. Everything under control. A lot of people would like to get away from Suriname right now. They're afraid things are going to get worse. Injustice and infraction of human rights. This is a very real experience to a lot of people nowadays, no wonder they're apprehensive. Still, at least something's being done about the corruption, which is so bad over here. That the same mistakes will be made all over again seems pretty likely. We'll have to wait and see. But I think they'll do a better job governing this place than we did. Time will tell. I'm giving this letter to Kees to be posted in Holland. Dear Oda Maria, till Friday or Saturday morning.

Love and kisses, Paul

COUNT YOUR BLESSINGS

Oda studies the words to blot out her sorrow and rage. The embroidered motto is the handiwork of the school principal's wife. She can't think of any blessings right now.

Eight o'clock, time to make her phone call. She's got the card in front of her. Oda lights a cigarette and dials the number. "Hello, Kiki, it's me. Oh, did I disturb you? Did I phone you already a while back? I'm sorry, Kiki. Yes, I'm fine. He'll be here any minute now. Yes, I'll get back to you. Yes, bye."

Oda buries her face in her hands. "Everybody's so selfish," she mutters. She gets up and walks through to the kitchen. Steps outside to switch on the terrace lights. Pauses to look at her own reflection. A transparent woman with a wide world inside her.

Oda rubs her hands. She raises the temperature on the thermostat. She must make the place welcoming, cozy. Light the floating candles. And the fire. There's still time to put a couple of towels in the washing machine. She draws the curtains in the master bedroom. From the window she can see the lights on at the neighbors' house. Inez or Hans is drawing the curtains of one of the first-floor windows. Oda perches on the bed and glances at the magazine lying on the bedside table: *The Green Beret.* On the cover a picture of twelve young paratroopers. Like fresh-faced boys receiving Holy Communion. In her bedroom she applies some day cream to her skin and changes a sanitary napkin, even though she isn't having a period. She puts it in one of the paper bags she steals from the supermarket and drops it in the trash under the washbasin. She feels a stab of pain behind her breastbone, goes downstairs, enters the study, lights up, there's another twinge, she must try to think of something else. Standing in front of the mirror in the alcove she brushes her hair. She checks the guest towels on the rack by the small washbasin in the downstairs bathroom. A clenched fist punches her breastbone from the inside. She goes into the kitchen and takes a plastic freezer bag out of a drawer. She seats herself at the table and breathes into the bag slowly and steadily, in, out, in, out, in, out.

Oda can feel there is someone behind her. She doesn't dare turn around. She tells herself she is imagining things. It can't be Henny, the wine merchant. The kitchen door is in full view. She wants to scream, but as in her nightmares, she can't utter a sound. Slowly she draws herself up, takes a deep breath. At the same time she feels his warm lips on her neck. She swings around and looks straight into the lieutenant colonel's eyes.

"I wanted to surprise you," he whispers, holding out the sprig of red blossom. "Here, some jungle flame, picked this morning by Bakabana."

He reaches for the plastic bag resting on the floor next to his shoes. "Papayas. You like them, don't you?"

Oda watches, speechless.

"And soursop, and passion fruit. And look, my sweet, fresh mangoes."

As if he had just slipped out to do some shopping.

"Will you come with me?"

A dark force grips her by the armpits, lifts her up, and drops her again. She sways, lists, recovers her balance in the lieutenant colonel's arms. Putting her mouth to his lips she feels as if the blood is draining from her body, her brain stops, for an instant she feels the way she always thought dogs–and other animals, too, for that matter–were capable of feeling: mindless and happy.

TWO

You climb the stairs you've climbed in your mind's eye night after night for the past few years, and at the top of the stairs you turn into the room on your right to find your wife lying on the double bed: the woman you'd spend the whole night with, as you would all the following days and nights, so you're going up those stairs carrying a heavy suitcase, in reality this time, and your desire grows with every tread, you've waited three years for this, have traveled halfway across the globe to get here— No, Klein, now that you're home at last you'll have cause to long for home with a vengeance, you're flooded with sentimental emotion already—when you reach the top, as you're about to enter the dream room on the right, you hear your wife's voice behind you on the stairs, and instead of mellifluous her voice sounds cool and strict: "To the left, Paul." Not that her voice was ever mellifluous, over the years it grew colder and colder until the day you knew it was over between you, you knew but you stayed. Eventually it occurred to you to accept a post overseas, because aside from the advantage of postponing your retirement for a couple of years and raising your pension, since years in the tropics count double, the real advantage was that you and she would not be together. You could no longer bear her excruciating, inhuman, constant aloofness, it had been hard enough having to share Vera with her, and when she was gone . . . you even suggested Oda come with you, but you knew she wouldn't and you hung your head cravenly until she said all right then, go if that's what you want, while going away was your dearest wish. You're a coward, Paul, sitting there on your terrace in faraway places gazing at the stars with a bottle of whiskey at your feet, imagining that things would turn out better, dreaming kitschy dreams full of sweetness and promise. People who spend their lives obeying orders end up out of touch, at night they have sudden fits of gloom or elation, they're weary and prone to

flashes of insight

memories

fears

desires.

At times like this people who spend their lives doing as they're told have a glass of whiskey and another and another and then fall into a deep sleep—again her voice telling you to turn left and first you look around in disbelief but she isn't there, then you glance fearfully at the door of Vera's room, which you thought you were too scared to set foot in ever again, and you shrink back to the middle of the landing.

"Left," she calls, "it's to the left!" But Paul turns right to catch a glimpse of the bedroom. The double bed has been halved, and the left mattress, the one on which he used to sleep, has been removed to make way for books and magazines.

"I just wanted to take a look," Paul says apologetically and turns to the left, to the other room. With his hand on the doorknob he looks over his shoulder. Oda is standing in the doorway of her bedroom, her arms crossed defensively. Paul pushes the door open slowly and Vera's world fans out before him: the red carpet, the print curtains, the red desk, the bed, his bedcover from Indonesia, his rocking chair. He's about to cross the threshold when he catches Oda's voice behind him announcing, "The master bedroom." Paul goes in and sets his suitcase on the floor by the little desk. The door swings shut behind him, making the Snoopy hanging from the key chain rattle against the wood. Paul screws up his eyes, the afterglow of the desk lamp lingers on his retina while Oda's footsteps descend the stairs. He begins to shiver, he must pull himself together, he opens his eyes and takes in the hand grenade lying on the desk, the brass cannon on the shelf, the bedside table with copies of *The Green Beret*, *The Times*, and *National Geographic*, the ledge bearing the little shield with the inscription LIEUTENANT COLONEL P. W. KLEIN, the books about

World War II and Indonesia, the pennants on the consoles, the bottle of Tabac Original aftershave lotion over the washbasin, the new Jordan toothbrush in the glass, the closet containing his old army uniforms and his civilian clothes: Paul Klein's civilian life starts right here in this girlish bedroom, which is now the master bedroom. He sits down at the desk and covers his eyes with his hands. Should he go back and ask if he can sleep with her? Does she want him to beg? Should he tell her he loves her and that he wasn't running away from the grief they shared, on the contrary, that he thought going away would make the grief bearable for both of them? It's not too late, he thinks hopefully, and he must tell her so. Paul gets up and opens the door, but on the landing he is overcome with the fear of her rejection, he can't stand it, he must put up his guard, stay in this torture chamber, sit out the punishment for a crime committed exclusively in her too-vivid imagination. When he stepped through the front door earlier on and took her in his arms she had been so soft and pliant, she was taken by surprise just as he was, she had kissed him and run her fingers over his neck, so what went wrong? A terrible sense of failure sweeps over him, he simply must stop his rampaging thoughts and go to sleep. He undresses next to the bed, hangs his smart tropical uniform in the closet, puts on his pajamas, brushes his teeth, washes his face with small circular movements, towels himself dry, and walks around the room. He hesitates by the bed, thinks of death and rape, pushes these thoughts away by telling himself that this bed is just a piece of furniture to sleep on. He must sleep. Paul sinks onto the bed, rolls over on his side, draws up his knees, and pillows his cheek on his folded hands. He thinks of all the things he can do in this room:

lie on the bed

stand

rock in the rocking chair

sit at the desk

lie on the floor and do exercises.

Paul can feel the eyes of the little dancing figures on the curtain boring into him, the blue, green, and red boys and girls holding hands in endless rows, an army of children staring at him, out of curiosity, out of pity, whatever, maybe they're trying to protect him–that would be nice–maybe they're there to protect him, the way Vera had protected him against Oda's temper in the old days, but maybe they're not, maybe they're laughing at him for being a failure, a clown in a girl's bed. Paul turns his back on them, draws up the duvet, and, shivering with cold and exhaustion, falls asleep at last.

THREE

*T*he next morning Paul stands ramrod-straight and motionless in his white pajamas between the little desk and his suitcase, gazing out the window. The frost on the thatch roof of Hans and Inez's house glistens in the low winter sun. It's uncomfortably warm in the room. Warmer than in Paramaribo at this hour. The air is dry. Oda always sets the thermostat too high. Paul would now be poised on his diving board, stretching his arms out sideways, flexing his knees, swinging his arms to the front, pushing off with the ball of his left foot, and diving into the pool. After one hundred laps he would rinse his body with ice-cold water and drink the fruit juices Bakabana had prepared for him. Papaya. Mango. Soursop. After that he would put on his immaculate khaki uniform, get into his air-conditioned Pontiac, and drive to the barracks under the waving palm trees.

Paul stretches out on the floor between the desk, the suitcase, and the bed. Lying on his back, knees raised, feet flat on the floor, he places his hands on his temples, brings his elbows close together, raises his upper body so that his shoulder blades come off the floor, and then lies back again. He gets through six sets of twenty inverted push-ups, breathing out as he rises, breathing in as he lies back. Then he stands up, squares his shoulders, puts his hands at the back of his waist, retracts his shoulder blades, bends over backward, holds that position briefly, lets his arms drop, slowly inclines forward, curving his spine and gently flexing his knees. This exercise is repeated nineteen times, after which he opens the door and walks to the bathroom. While urinating he adjusts the venetian blinds with one hand and looks out at the bare winter garden. He notices Hans driving past in his car. Hans is a working man. Paul returns to his room and slips into his bathrobe. The door to Oda's bedroom is shut. Paul goes downstairs. In the kitchen he finds the breakfast table laid for him. Oda always sets the table in the evening. She doesn't like putting things off. She has even filled the coffeemaker with water and coffee. The tray with her plate, cup, and glass is ready by the sink. Paul takes the loaf out of the bread box, sets butter and jam on the table, drops two slices in the toaster, and takes a seat. He looks out the window, sees a blue tit clinging to the string of peanuts Oda has tied between the nesting box and the rowan tree. While the bird attacks a peanut it darts him a look of complicity. Why not have breakfast together? Paul eats his two pieces of toast with jam, drinks his two cups of strong coffee, peels his apple. A plump ginger tomcat steals through the flower beds. The blue tit takes flight and perches on the balcony railing. Paul looks at the clock over the door. Ten o'clock. He squeezes some oranges for Oda, butters some toast, pours coffee into her cup. He carries the breakfast tray upstairs and leaves it on the floor outside her door. He takes a shower, shaves, and gets dressed. Corduroys, shirt, lamb's-wool sweater. Fastening his belt he is pleased to find he has not gained weight. He puts on his shoes and goes downstairs. Wearing a thick winter coat he steps out of the front door, holds his hands behind his back, and strolls around the house, inspecting the trees, the herbaceous borders, the lawn. Oda's foresters, as she calls her gardeners, have pruned heavily. He surveys the bicycles in the shed and takes a quick look at the motorcycle under the gray plastic shroud. Oda has left everything untouched. He goes down to the mailbox at the bottom of the drive, takes out the newspaper and the mail. No letters for him. He mounts the stairs, puts the newspaper and the mail on the floor by Oda's door where he left the tray earlier, and goes into his room. He settles down in his rocking chair, resting his feet on the wooden crossbar. He opens the November issue of *The Green Beret* and starts reading the obituaries. His eyes skim the mug shots of old and young paratroopers, who died after a courageously borne illness or passed away suddenly or peacefully or tragically or far too young, after a brave struggle or a short illness, much-loved and admired and cherished fathers, dearly beloved sons, sadly missed husbands, or simply deceased. After that Paul browses through the columns headed BIRTHS, NEW POSTINGS, PROMOTED, HONORS, and RETIRED FROM SERVICE. Finally he reads the "Commando Chronicle," which is devoted to the glories and adversities marking the recent but colorful history of the Select Commando Corps. On the following page the dates are given for the next reunion. In a few weeks' time he'll see his army buddies again, perhaps they'll do some marching. Oda's lying low. She'll break her silence at the least expected moment for maximum effect, strike fear into him as he rises to face her with a look of terror in his eyes, and she'll say, Doing nothing as usual?–and for an instant he'll hope that this signals the start of a proper conversation, but the door slams shut and her strident heels descend the stairs.

He'll stay in his room for the rest of the day because his wife wants to be left alone. He might venture downstairs once she has driven off, though. It's time to read the paper and drink tea. When Oda returns he'll open the garage door for her and carry the shopping inside and pour her a glass of whiskey. He'll have a Dutch gin himself. After that he'd better take his glass and the bottle upstairs, because she gets distracted from her cooking when he's around. Eventually she'll ring the brass bell summoning Paul to the kitchen, she'll dish out the food, and he'll say, "You're such a wonderful cook, Oda," before he's even tasted it, whereupon she'll take her plate into the living room (she gets at you, you get at her) and lie down on the sofa to watch television. He'll do the dishes and bring her a cup of coffee. He'll sit at the other end of the sofa and watch television, too, at least that'll be one thing they can share, but soon he'll feel tired, why not go to bed early–tomorrow's another day–and he'll go upstairs, take a shower, put on his pajamas, get into bed, turn off the light, and fall asleep. Sleep is one of Paul's main blessings. He's a good sleeper, so good as to be oblivious to his wife's nocturnal habits.

Paul has the place to himself in the mornings. He does his exercises, has breakfast, leaves the tray outside Oda's door along with the newspaper. She takes them inside, shuts the door, and doesn't emerge until after Paul has had his lunch, has run her a bath, and has retired to his room. After her bath she gets dressed. Then she gets in her car and drives off. When she returns Paul opens the garage, carries the shopping inside, pours her a glass of whiskey and himself some Dutch gin. To dull their senses a little.

This is not living. This is a deadlock. You've got to get your act together, you've got to leave her, you've got to take your life in your hands, because she won't tell you to go, that's not her style, she'll do all she can to convince you that it was your idea . . . You must get up, leave this room, go down the stairs, out the front door, down the drive, into the world.

The door swings open to reveal an extended arm, that's all he can see before the door shuts again, making Snoopy rattle against the wood. Oda's awake! Paul runs after her and tries to put his arms around her, "Oda, I love you!" But she wrenches his hands off her waist. "Leave me alone," she cries. Paul returns to his room, settles down in his rocking chair, and rocks.

FOUR

*A*ll this rocking in his rocking chair with his feet on the wooden crossbar, bumpety-bump against the closet door, all this waiting, or rather all the lying on his back with his legs over the foot of the bed, or on his side with drawn-up knees, indeed all the sitting at the little desk with his legs crammed into the space underneath and his knees pushed against the wall at the back, all these things give him a caged feeling. That's how Oda wants him to feel, it's not only that she's saying, I'm out here and you're in there, but also, You're your own prisoner. It's six or seven days since he returned, not that it makes any difference. Paul thinks back to the last evening he spent in this house before his departure three years ago. When the green van arrived to pick him up, Oda had walked him down the drive, she'd gotten on top of one of the border stones and had waved and waved, glad to see him go, she'd waved him goodbye, away, off, out of her life. The driver had remarked that he must be sorry to be leaving, the poor man was attracted to her, everyone was attracted to her, she was charming, Paul's wife was the mascot of the barracks, she was regarded with incredulity and admiration by officers and men alike. Oda was beautiful, elegant, stylish, incomparably more so than all the other army wives, she smoked, she drank, she pulled faces behind people's backs, no doubt behind his, too, she fired the starting pistol at track races (and held the pistol to her head), she performed the ceremonial kickoff at soccer matches (dangling her high-heeled shoes from her hand), she told entertaining stories, a cigarette in one hand and a glass in the other . . . He thought he must be the biggest fool on earth to leave her like this, but he had no choice. Oda did not turn her charm on him. The look in her eyes chilled him to the bone. All the way to the airport he sat stiffly behind the driver without saying a word.

Paul's rocking again, bumping against the closet. He's holding a present from Hans and Inez in his hands. WEL-COME HOME, it says on the card attached to the string. The wrapping paper is patterned with winter scenes in oval frames. One of the little pictures is of a pair of gnomes wearing red caps and mittens, with a sled in the snow, one pulling, the other pushing, a pair of robins looking on; the sled is piled with parcels tied with ribbons and a basket of apples as rosy as the gnomes' cheeks. Another picture shows a gnome sitting in the snow with a fawn on his lap, gazing at a candle on a tree trunk; there's also a fox, a long-eared white rabbit, a squirrel sitting on the gnome's satchel, and several yellow birds on an overhanging branch. Paul puts his foot against the desk to stop rocking. Although he had meant to wait until Christmas, he tears the wrapping paper off and drops it on the floor beside him. His gift is a bottle made of frosted glass with a red metal top. Beneath an arch formed by the letters WODKA the glass is transparent, creating an oval peephole. Peering through the clear glass, Paul can see the silhouettes of three figures around a table. They've got wigs on, and shoes with buckles. The left figure leans back in a chair, smoking a long-stemmed pipe. The middle one is seated at the table, a similar pipe in one hand and a glass in the other. The one on the right is on his feet, raising a toast. Paul unscrews the red cap and sniffs at the contents. He takes a gulp, and another. He leans back and closes his eyes. He raises the bottle to his mouth again. His throat is on fire. Paul gets up from the rocking chair and stumbles to the chair by the desk. He sets the bottle in front of him and opens the top drawer. He takes out an exercise book and scrutinizes it in the light of the desk lamp. On the front there's a drawing of a chick emerging from its egg. The remaining piece of shell on its head is inscribed with curly letters:

Vera Maria Klein
Vera Alexandra Maria Klein
Alexandra Maria Klein
Alexandra Klein

as if to mark the gradual transformation of one little girl into another. Paul opens the exercise book and reads the first page.

> We are making an autumn wood. First we planted some trees. We all stood around the table with sand on top. Everybody wanted to give something. Mario gave some deer. We need more trees. Today we will bring more trees to school. We also put a bird's egg in our wood. There are fairies in our wood. We all have a bit of the wood to make the way we like. We all think it will look very nice.

Paul leafs through the exercise book. Dictations and rows of words. Some pages are decorated with little stenciled cartoons: a boy lying in front of a tent, a girl with a butterfly net. She got a bad grade for her last dictation. There were a lot of spelling mistakes. Perhaps she'd been daydreaming. What had his little girl been dreaming about? He shuts the book and takes another swig from the bottle. Then he rummages in the drawer and takes out a folder with a gray cover bearing the title ALL TOGETHER, in Vera's handwriting. The letters are very big, each of them filled in with a different color. There are also pictures of flowers, and a sun. A baby Jesus colored bright pink with a marker pen, the hair canary yellow. Her name in curly letters. Paul opens the folder. The top sheet has two photographs pasted on it.

The first is a large color photograph of Oda, Vera, and Emil around the barbecue in the garden. Oda is kneeling with a cigarette in one hand and a skewer of meat cubes in the other; she's wearing fawn trousers, a black short-sleeved top, a brooch in the shape of her initial O, sunglasses, a black headband. To her right Vera in a red pantsuit, laying a skewer threaded with marshmallows on the barbecue. Emil on his knees behind her, uncorking a bottle of wine. Paul's shadow falls across the threesome.

The second is a small black-and-white snapshot. It was taken by Oda and shows Vera and Paul in front of the tower. Vera eyes the camera with alarm, clinging to her dad's winter coat with both hands. As though she wants him to rescue her.

Paul takes the gray folder and his bottle and settles down in the rocking chair again. The next sheet is a poem entitled "Xmas Carols." He takes another swig and starts reading. *And in thy deep and dreamless sleep / The silent stars go by. / Yet in thy dark streets shineth / The everlasting light. / The hopes and fears of all the years / Are met in thee tonight.* His eyes go back to *The hopes and fears of all the years.* He drinks some more, his rocking chair bumps against the closet, his head reels, one, two, one, two, he's rocking into a new world, one, two, one, two, another sip and read on . . . *As with gladness men of old / Did the guiding star behold. / As with joy they hailed its light / Leading onward, beaming bright.* He hears bells pealing–no, the bells are tolling as the mourners gather, his army colleagues, her classmates, one, two, one, two, he feels as empty as the bell, the emptiness within his shell of armor rocks back and forth soundlessly, it is the hush of the void. He's falling apart, tears are stinging in his eyes. "Oda," he mumbles, "Oda," but he has no strength in his throat, he bites his lips, struggles to control himself. *As with joy they hailed its light / Leading onward, beaming bright.* "Light," Paul echoes, "light, light." *As with gladness men of old / Did the guiding star behold.* "I knew it," he mumbles, "there was the child, and the child was the guiding star." He is singing now. "And they hailed its light." His voice rises to a scream: "Light! Light! Command Light!"

The pattern on the curtain comes alive, beaming luridly into the red room, the boys and girls singing and lurching in fluorescent rows, performing torch dances before his very eyes. Paul tries to rise from the rocking chair, his arms reaching out to the light, one, two, up we go. The door behind him flies open and Paul turns around, shielding his face with his hands. "There's a fire!" Oda yells.

Paul follows Oda down the stairs, through the hall, past the kitchen, into the garden; he follows her across the herbaceous border, gets down to crawl through the hole in the fence after her, heads toward a gigantic conflagration. They huddle behind a bush near the swimming pool, flames leap up from the roof and windows, a great roar fills the air, the world is quaking, their clothes flap wildly in the high wind, there are screams, voices, high-pitched, unintelligible, streaks of yellow, livid tongues of fire, showers of sparks. They see their neighbors watching as their house burns down. Hans restrained by a fireman, his arms outstretched to the fire, Inez staring wide-eyed at the attic collapsing onto the first floor. Paul is too drunk to do anything, nor indeed has he any desire to take action, it's enough for him to see the fire and feel Oda's body close to his. She lays her head on his shoulder, puts her arm around his waist, the cries subside into sighs and sobs. Hans and Inez are tinged with pink against the plumes of black smoke, silhouettes of despair on the edge of a glowing mass, it's as if the voices rising to make themselves heard over the fire blend into a single, primeval tone. Then, quite suddenly, there's a girl with a blanket around her shoulders, stepping gingerly across the cold grass, swinging her head from side to side, white-faced, frightened. Her eyes meet his fleetingly. Paul wants to go to her, but Oda's fingers are running over his spine.

PART 3

P aul's ablaze, he can't think or act, just lets himself be swung around and around, spun like a top, no, it's not that, it's the world that's spinning . . . the shrubs, the trees, the burning house, the stars, and the night all wheeling around him at great speed. He doubles up, clutching his head with his hands for fear that it'll fly off and whiz around his trunk like a planet, head and heart divided forevermore; his feet planted apart on the ground no longer seem to belong to him. This can't be real, the flames, the girl, Oda's head on his shoulder, her breath on his neck. His legs give way, he falls over backward, draws up his knees, and hugs them to his chest so he won't lose them. "It's the reckoning!" she cries triumphantly, "the day of reckoning." He feels he's in one of those dreams where you can't move although you must, where things change shape while you crave the sound of a human voice, and he tries saying "I love you, I love you," but he can't, his voice falters, the words stick in his throat. "It's all right," she purrs, "we're going home now." But first the world has to stop turning . . . the burning house, the bushes, the trees, the plumes of smoke in the moonlight reassemble in their rightful positions. He reaches out to her, lets her take his hand and scoop him away from here, the two of them together making a dash for it like schoolchildren caught playing with matches, back home through the bushes, the hole in the fence, the herbaceous border, across the lawn, into the house. She pulls him after her up the stairs to the room in which every night, in his mind's eye . . . "Come on, come on," she cries, "I want you, come to bed, pull my boots off, we're safe here in our downy burrow, come on, Paul, it feels good here, so fucking good, I've been so lonely, so brave . . ." He's stunned, can't keep up with her, feels her thighs and breasts as she wraps herself around him so tightly he can't breathe. She pulls down his zipper, fumbles in his pants, hurts him. Then he breaks away, draws himself up at the foot of the bed, and grabs hold of the boot she, lying on her back, extends to him. "Easy now, Oda," he whispers. He pulls hard and crashes against the closet, still holding the boot in his hands, draws himself up again. Now for the other boot. He pulls it off, unsheathing her leg; she's got great legs, every man can see these legs are great. He kicks off his shoes, strips off his pants, shirt, and socks, and lies down beside her. "All right, love?" her voice comes back to him, "we're going home," and the whole world spins around again: Oda, the house, the bushes, the trees, the plumes of smoke in the moonlight. He reaches out to her, lets her take him by the hand and lead him wherever she pleases.

IN THE YEARS BEFORE HE LEFT THEY would sleep in the same bed, on separate mattresses, with their backs to each other. She was resolved not to let him near her, if his hand or foot strayed too close she would tell him to keep to his own half, but he made no attempt to go near her: he had an exasperating way of keeping his distance, a paragon of resignation. She thinks it was just a matter of being sensible as far as he was concerned, a bed being somewhere to sleep and tomorrow being another day when he would rise early and have the place to himself. He would put on his uniform, set the breakfast tray down by the door, and leave to do goodness knows what–jog, go for a bike ride, fence with his army buddies or whatever, and when he was not engaging in sports he would no doubt be taking stock of his pairs of socks, trousers, helmets, cannons. A man in a man's world. Order and armor made up his survival strategy. Order, armor, and routine. His uniform was his shield, the outer shell protecting his bare skin. Oda had to peel off layer after layer to get through to him, but it was all in vain because his bare skin was armored, too; her words bounced right off, as did the blows from her fists, the lashes from her whip.

. . .

As he gave Oda no cause to rebuff him, her rage found no issue. She was left to stew in her own juices. She seethed and thought, Why are we together? She knew the answer. It had nothing to do with him, he was blameless, it was all her own doing. She could hear him think, She'll get over it, time works wonders; and she detested his naïve confidence. Time doesn't work wonders, time doesn't do a thing, except maybe grin maliciously, because she is at his mercy and he knows full well that if he sends her packing she will be finished.

IT'S AS IF PILES ARE BEING DRIVEN into his head. His mouth is parched. He observes her face, the creases by the temples, the dyed hair showing gray at the roots, the smudged mascara, the specks of saliva at the corners of her mouth. He's afraid it'll turn out to have been nothing but a fit of drunkenness, that when she awakes she'll push him away, but then she opens her eyes (bright, clear, unsurprised, as if they've been watching him through closed eyelids all the time) and says his name, draws him close. He puts off going to the bathroom for fear that she'll have changed her mind by the time he comes back, that she won't have him. He doesn't dare say a word, let alone ask a question. But when she goes to the bathroom he follows her to the door, watches her sit on the toilet staring into the dark garden, and after her he goes, too, and she waits and watches him urinate the way she sometimes did long ago, and together they go back, past Vera's room, get into bed again, nestle up close to each other. He feels her head between his legs, his penis in her mouth, he thought this would never happen again, nor will it ever happen again . . . she seems determined, he's scared she'll bite.

THE ROAD IS STREWN WITH BROKEN branches and leaves, the weather cold and blustery. An empty plastic bag swirls phantomlike before Oda's windshield. Hans and Inez's drive is choked with vehicles. Police, fire department, municipal demolition team. Oda parks in the road. It has just started to rain when she gets out of her car. The smell of a log fire. A family smell. Clasping the collar of her coat with one hand and holding an umbrella in the other she walks up to the house. A collapsed skeleton. Black. The wind blows through the empty carcass. A police officer tells her the owners have gone to the Juliana Hotel. Does he know what caused the fire, she asks. He shakes his head. It started in the roof, apparently. They're conducting an investigation.

Oda contemplates the devastation, then turns away. She feels pity and also a tingle of excitement. She gets in her car and drives to the hotel. She hasn't been back there since the funeral and the condolences when she had stood at Paul's side, unseeing and unfeeling, shaking hands with people.

Hans and Inez are in the breakfast room facing each other across one of the tables. Hans says, "It's not the end of the world." Inez takes his hand absently. She looks wan.

"Have you lost everything?" Oda asks.

"We were able to rescue a couple of paintings," Hans replies.

"Where's your young friend?"

"Daisy's asleep," Inez mumbles.

"Imagine being in a foreign country surrounded by strangers, and on your second night the house you're staying in burns down," Hans says.

"That must be terrible."

"Traumatic," Inez adds.

"Why don't you . . ." Oda hardly dares to finish her sentence. "You could come and stay with us, you know. We can make room in the attic."

"It's better if we stay here," Inez explains. "We've got a lot to sort out. Find another house, for one thing."

"What about the girl?"

"She might want to go back to the States. She's had a terrible shock. She's only fifteen."

"She could . . . she could come and stay with us. I mean, we'd do everything to make her feel welcome." Oda is stammering as if it's an indecent proposal.

"But . . ."

"Honestly, it's no problem at all. Paul and I have plenty of time on our hands."

"You'd better ask her yourself," says Inez.

"Let's go to her room," Hans suggests.

Oda follows Hans through the lobby, up the stairs to

the first floor, and along the landing with the spinning wheel, the copper pans on the wall, and the dried flower arrangement. He knocks at room number 5. The door opens a crack. She glimpses a white unicorn and above it two flashing eyes.

PAUL HAS BEEN GAZING INTO THE dark for the past half hour. Maybe an hour. He tells himself it's fine with me if it's what Oda wants, which it is. He's not at liberty to contradict her. She didn't give him any opportunity to do so, anyway. There was something in her tone when she announced: "Her name's Daisy!" She could have been saying "We're calling her Daisy," the way you might if you had a new baby or a puppy from the animal shelter. Paul's initial reaction had been all wrong. He'd said, "But we're together again at last." Oda had glared at him with white-hot eyes. How could he be so heartless? And then he'd made matters worse by venturing to ask how long she'd be staying. "You don't ask someone you've just invited to stay when they'll be leaving, that would be ghastly," she'd said, and that was that. He thought he'd ruined everything now, and that she'd order him back to his kennel, and he'd said, "All right, ask her. Maybe . . ." She'd thrown her arms around his neck and hugged him. "It's all right," she'd whispered in his ear. He knew everything would be all right so long as everything was done her way. He has misgivings. Oda thinks she knows what she's doing, but in fact she's impulsive. There's nothing to stop her turning into an ice queen from one moment to the next.

The familiar sound of Oda's car. Paul crosses the hall to open the front door. White face, pale eyes, shy smile, long dark hair, little feather earrings. There's something familiar about Daisy. She's wearing Oda's sheepskin coat and he notices his own old green checkered scarf around her neck. In her hand a plastic bag. Oda ushers her inside and shuts the door. He takes Daisy's coat. She looks around the hall, rubbing her hands. She's wearing Oda's running shoes and dark blue tracksuit. She runs her finger over the alligator on the hat rack, slips her pinkie between the sharp little teeth lining the gaping jaws. "He's cute," she says hoarsely, stroking its head.

Paul goes upstairs carrying Daisy's plastic bag. Oda and Daisy follow behind. The three of them stand in Vera's room. Oda switches the desk lamp on.

"Red, my favorite color," Daisy says. "We don't have any red in our home, my parents don't like it." She stoops to smell the roses in the vase on her bedside table. "It's really very sweet of you."

PAUL IS ON HIS KNEES BY THE HEARTH putting a log on the fire. Oda strikes a match to light the candles. Daisy is bending over the cabinet. She points to a photograph of Vera on a swing. "Who's that?"

"Vera, our little girl," Oda replies.

"She drowned in the summer of 1973," Paul adds, poking the fire.

Daisy settles herself on the sofa. She is holding the photograph in her hands. Oda sits down beside her and puts her arm around the girl's shoulders while they look at Vera on the swing, plunging forward with out-stretched legs. Oda is in the background, her arms raised to give the next push.

"Do you have any more children?" Daisy asks carefully.

Oda and Vera were connected like the sea and the shore. Whenever Vera retreated Oda would lie vast and flat under the sky, when Vera advanced again Oda would allow herself to be flooded, lapped, erased, this perpetual motion between mother and child . . . but without a child it is always ebb tide, the sea retreats for good and the shore lies there waiting although it should know better, waiting out of sheer habit, perhaps, or because it cannot help itself.

Having a child is what binds you to the world, Oda once heard a voice say on the radio. How apt, she had thought. Once Vera was born she no longer felt the need to punish the world for everything she had not become. Henceforth her world was the world of her child. When Vera died, Oda had to turn the saying around: Losing a child cuts you off from the world. From then on Oda merely drifted, surprised that her feet actually touched the ground, although the ground was adrift, too, supposedly without direction but secretly in search of something to live for.

Daisy has been asleep for fourteen hours. Should they bring her tea in bed? Or would she prefer coffee? How long do fifteen-year-old girls usually sleep anyway? "Shall we begin?" Paul proposes.

"Let's wait," Oda says. "If she comes down to find we've already had breakfast she won't feel welcome."

Paul gets up and walks out into the garden. He looks up at Daisy's room.

"Calm down, for goodness' sake," Oda calls, motioning him to come inside.

Paul pours the coffee. Oda lights a cigarette and stares out the window. They hear a door closing, taps running. Oda gets up from the table. Paul follows her into the hall. She goes up the stairs. Comes down again. "She's gone back to her room," Oda says in a low, rueful voice.

Oda and Paul are sitting opposite each other without speaking. Paul scrapes the burned edges off his toast with his knife. The kitchen door is open. They listen to every sound. Oda stands up, sighs, and says she must go shopping.

"Why don't you wait a bit," Paul suggests.

"I can't, the shops close at noon."

While Oda puts on her coat she says she's looking forward to telling the butcher she wants three steaks. She knows he will say, "Did you say *three*, Mrs. Klein?"

Paul eats his toast with jam. She could come downstairs any moment now. He'll ask her what she'd like to drink. Whether she slept well. What she dreamed about. He clears away his plate and sets the table for Daisy. He sits down again and waits. Quarter of an hour, half an hour, an hour. He hears Oda's car pulling up. He opens the garage door and lifts the shopping bags out of the trunk.

"This is too much," Oda says when she sees Daisy hasn't had her breakfast yet.

"Perhaps she's shy."

Footsteps on the stairs. Oda and Paul exchange anxious looks. Daisy appears in the kitchen. Barefoot. A sweatshirt over her nightgown. "Good morning," she says timidly.

"Did you sleep well?" Oda asks.

"Very well."

"Did you have any dreams?"

"I dreamed that I was flying, all night long."

"What would you like to drink?" asks Paul.

"Just some water, please."

He turns to the sink and holds a glass under the tap. They watch as Daisy raises the glass to her lips with both hands and takes a first sip. She is wearing a ring with a skull.

"Have something to eat," Oda says.

"I'm not hungry."

Oda puffs nervously on her cigarette. She's still wearing her coat.

"Have some fruit then," Paul says in a fatherly tone. He peels an apple for her the way he used to do for Vera. He passes the quarters to Daisy, who puts them in her mouth one by one.

ODA HAS PUT OUT A NAIL FILE, a bowl of warm water, an orange stick, a hoof stick, and nail clippers on the dressing table. She is holding Daisy's hands in hers. Finely shaped, with long fingers. The horrible ring. Daisy points to a mark on the ball of her thumb.

"It's a tattoo my brother made," she says, "with a ballpoint pen. Five years ago."

Oda lays Daisy's hands on her lap and starts filing the nails.

"My brother's even worse than me. He gets thrown out of every school they send him to. I had some pictures of him. Too bad they got burned."

Daisy follows every movement Oda makes. She asks, "Why don't you just cut them?"

"They're smoother and better-shaped if you use a file. And they don't split as easily. Metal files give you hangnails. Emery boards are better."

She puts Daisy's hands in the bowl to soak in the warm water, to which she has added some lemon juice. She takes the pointed end of the orange stick and scrapes it under the nails, then removes the bits of dead skin along the cuticles first with a pair of little scissors and then with the clippers. She rubs cream all over the girl's hands. Using the hoof stick she pushes back the cuticles along the base of the nails. She asks if she'd like some nail polish. Daisy bursts out laughing. She's laughing at Oda. She flops onto the bed on her stomach and opens a magazine. Her legs swing up and down. Oda lights a cigarette. Daisy wants one, too.

"When I apply for a new passport, can I tell them any name I like?"

"I shouldn't think so. Perhaps you could change your first name. You'd better ask Paul."

"Okay."

"Which name would you choose?"

"I don't know, Alexandra maybe." She turns over on her back and folds her arms behind her head.

HOW OFTEN HAD HE MISTAKEN OTHER girls for his own daughter in the old days! A glimpse of a girl swerving dangerously on a bicycle, a girl being led away by two strangers, girls in places where they had no business being. Each time it made his heart lurch. Each time he realized his error, he was amazed at the workings of his mind. How could he possibly confuse the one he loved most of all with someone else?

Daisy is standing by the entrance to the army base. He has to force himself to think of her as Daisy. He used to come here often with Vera. She loved wandering around on the base on her afternoons off from school, she loved the attention she got from the soldiers. Paul

83

could rest assured, his daughter was the best-guarded little girl in the world.

They stroll down the narrow sandy path with the barbed wire on one side and the woods on the other. Daisy slips her arm through his. "What do they keep in those sheds?" she asks, pointing to the hangars on the other side of the barbed wire.

"Ammunition."

"And what else?"

"Motor oil."

"And what else?"

He replies: "Pillows, blankets, camp beds, uniforms, helmets, caps, berets, shirts, shoes, socks, underwear . . ."

"Enough for all the soldiers in Holland?"

"Yes."

"How wonderful!" she cries gleefully.

Paul tells Daisy about the rabbit hutch he built for Vera in the carpentry workshop at the army base. It was shaped like a farmhouse and it had a green roof and green shutters and a little gangway to the door. The last time they'd gone away on vacation they'd taken Bugs and Bunny and the whole rabbit farm to the base, to be looked after by the soldiers. They'd left the hutch in the middle of the grass circle by the gate. Right in front of the Dutch flag. Vera had stood up on the backseat to wave goodbye to her rabbits. The barrier had come down, the gates had closed, the sentry had raised his hand in farewell. Paul feels a lump in his throat. Daisy takes his hand in hers. The path heads away from the fence into the woods. A thin veil of mist on the ground, leafless treetops dark against the gray sky. Daisy asks, "Where do you think she is now?" Paul keeps his eyes fixed ahead, searching for an answer. The mist thickens, a soft rain begins to fall. Daisy leans close against his shoulder.

Later, in the car on the way home, she asks, "Will you take me for a ride on your motorcycle sometime?"

"On my motorcycle?"

"Yes, that thing under the plastic sheet in the shed."

"It's years since I rode it."

"Why?"

"Oda didn't approve."

"I always do what I like anyway."

"The best bike ride of my life was in the States."

"When was that?"

"In 1954."

"That's a very long time ago for a best bike ride."

Daisy fiddles with the buttons on the car radio. None of the stations appeal to her. She starts singing "Bat Out Of Hell."

Her hand rests against his neck. Paul can't decide whether it's the hand of a child or a woman, of a daughter or a girlfriend. He tries to banish these thoughts from his mind. They are inappropriate.

I'M A BAT OUT OF HELL, SWOOPING over the graves to the howl of sirens, the roar of flames, there's evil in the night and thunder in the air, the night is red and the thunder is dead, if she has to be damned, she wants to be damned, the idea that *she* should be lying in bed in this room instead of her . . . She'd woken up in the morning, opened these very curtains, perhaps she'd sat at the little desk for a moment, then she'd gotten dressed, gone downstairs to have breakfast with Paul, and she'd left the house never to return.

The state you leave your room in when you die is what remains for the bereaved to contemplate. The pencil you leave lying around will be touched by their eyes. Suddenly the pencil itself and the place where it lies take on a special meaning. Their eyes take the pencil and attach it to your hand and your hand to your arm, your shoulders, your head, your trunk, your legs; they can see you sitting at your desk holding that pencil in your hand, drawing the last picture you will ever draw, they see you rising from your desk and lying down on the bed, they see you getting up, crossing to the balcony door, and stepping outside, they see you coming in again and they call your name, but there is no answer because you are dead. They see the pencil lying on the desk, exactly where you left it, and you will never come back.

Like a bat out of hell. The figures on the curtains all sprout wings in the night and leap astride their motorcycles, and together we rise over the graves in a great column, you understand, and we fly through hell.

. . .

86

That afternoon she had gone to the Juliana Hotel to deliver a box of chocolates from Oda for Hans and Inez. She saw Inez sitting by the window in the lounge, facing a man in a suit, whom she hadn't seen before. The table between them was piled with documents. Suddenly she was terrified they were going to tell her she'd have to go home. She didn't want to be sent away. She crossed the street to the cemetery. At the entrance she hesitated. She opened the box and ate the chocolates one by one as she wandered past the graves. She paused a bit longer at the graves of young people than at those of people who died in old age. She stood still a long time at the grave of a sixteen-year-old girl. Her name was Irma, or something like that. Nearby she came across Vera's grave. A few rocks, a tiny pond, wild strawberries. Suddenly she felt horribly nauseous. She ran back toward the exit, because you can't very well barf all over someone's grave. She threw up the chocolates on a heap of refuse and dead flowers. She saw an old woman eyeing her with pity. Then she walked back to the house. There was no one there.

FOOTSTEPS ON THE STAIRS. IT IS Paul, coming up with another trophy he has fished out of the moving crate.

"What do you suppose it'll be this time?" Oda asks. Daisy is lying next to her on Paul's side of the bed. She is wearing her unicorn T-shirt.

"A golf bag?"

"A safari hat?"

"A mosquito net?"

Not a sound.

"Where is he?"

"Paul!" Daisy shouts. "Don't keep us waiting."

Silence.

"This is very boring," Oda calls to him. She lights a cigarette.

Suddenly there is an apparition at the door: a monstrous head with pointed teeth and goggle eyes. A huge crocodile comes lurching into the room. Daisy lets out a scream.

"You haven't . . ."

"Yes, I have. An alligator."

"But we've got one already!" Oda cries.

"No, that one's a baby gator, this is the father," Paul says. The reptile has marbles for eyes and its jaws are lined with red plastic. "My neighbor and I shot him behind our house."

"Go away, I don't want you in my room."

"It's my room, too, sweetheart. This gator has just as much right to be here as you."

"But it's *my* birthday!" Oda cries.

Daisy buries her head under the duvet, squeaking with excitement.

"You can come out now, Daisy," Paul teases, brandishing the alligator.

Daisy pulls her head out from under the cover and starts yelling when Paul swings the creature in her direction.

"This one's for you," Paul says. "Oda doesn't want it."

"Go away," Daisy cries.

Paul growls, bares his teeth, rolls his eyes. Oda has never seen him like that. Daisy rushes out of the room with Paul giving chase, they run up the stairs, there is stamping, shouting, shrieking in the attic overhead, then they come down again. The two of them collapse breathlessly on the bed. Paul's hand rests on Daisy's leg. Oda shoots her a challenging look.

"Anything wrong?" asks Daisy.

"Nothing, love," says Oda.

Paul makes to crawl under the duvet next to Oda.

"And now you've got to go," Oda says.

He stands up and marches out of the bedroom with the alligator under his arm. Daisy turns to Oda with a smile. She says, "Now I'm all yours."

"HAVE YOU SEEN *THE GLASS MENAGERIE*?" Oda asks Daisy. "It's by Tennessee Williams."

"No, I haven't."

"It's his most famous play."

"Actually, I have no idea what you're talking about. You can't expect me to know everything, Oda."

"The girl in the play is lonely. She's crippled or something. She collects glass animals. Her favorite is a unicorn made of crystal. One day the young man she's in love with comes to visit. When she shows him her prize possession he drops it by accident, and it breaks."

"What a jerk."

"She doesn't mind about the unicorn, though, because she loves him and she thinks he loves her, too."

"He ought to get her a new one."

"But it was the only one of its kind."

"Too bad."

"The young man turns out to be in love with another woman and the girl is left behind with her broken unicorn."

"How sad."

"Yes, especially for the girl's mother."

"Why was it so bad for the mother–the unicorn didn't belong to her, did it?"

"She had pinned all her hopes on him being the right man for her daughter."

"Was she in love with him herself, by any chance?"

"I don't think so."

"What a story."

"For some parents the happiness of their child is the most important thing in the world."

ODA'S GOOD HUMOR IS A TRAP. Paul walks right into it. She lures him to her side only to slam the door in his face. Why is he so gullible? Because he loves her, all he wants is to love her, he wants to love her every minute they are together: wholeheartedly, unabashedly, totally.

They were at the restaurant, sitting at their old table by the window. They hadn't been back there since Vera died. Paul sat facing the two women. Daisy wore Oda's little black dress. Her long hair swept her bare shoulders. She was gorgeous. In her ears she wore the gold bars he'd given Oda years ago for her fortieth birthday. Oda wore her white silk blouse and Daisy's feather earrings. She'd put her hair up. He watched their hands, their eyes, their mouths as they chatted and smiled. He feasted his eyes on them. He was proud of his attractive companions. Oda was relaxed. The food was excellent. After dessert Paul suggested inviting Emil to join them for a drink.

"What put that idea into your head?" Oda said, startled.

"I haven't seen him since I got back."

"Who's Emil?" asked Daisy.

"He's my buddy."

"Buddy?"

"His friend," said Oda.

"A buddy is not the same as a friend," Paul said. "Buddies are not necessarily your friends."

"So what's the difference?"

"Buddies help you in need, even if they don't particularly like you."

"But don't you like Emil?"

"He's a buddy whom I like as a friend, too. We've gone through a lot together."

"They go back a very long way," Oda explained.

"It would be nice if he could join us. He lives just up the road."

"And do you like him, too?" Daisy asked Oda.

"I haven't seen him for ages."

"He used to come to the house a lot," Paul said.

"Is he in the army, too?" asked Daisy.

"He's a general."

"I'd like to meet him sometime."

"Not tonight," Oda said firmly. "It's my birthday." Oda pressed her fingers to her temples and stared icily into the distance. "Let's go," she said, rising from the table. A few minutes later all three of them were out in the street.

It was a beautiful evening. Cold and clear. Paul suggested taking a stroll along the river and then having a drink in the Floris Café. Oda said she was not in the mood. They drove home in silence. Oda went straight upstairs. Daisy and Paul sat facing each other at the kitchen table. "This is gruesome," Daisy said morosely. In the harsh light she looked terrifying. She was wearing white face powder. Red lipstick. False eyelashes that cast spiky shadows under her eyes. Like tiny crabs.

"DOWN WITH MEN," ODA HAD CRIED when she was a girl, whipping her belt around in wild circles. She kept others at a distance. She ran headlong into the world. Who was she imitating? Maybe an actor she had seen onstage. Why that and not something else? Why did cracking a whip impress her more deeply than, say, ballet? Maybe she thought of dancing as a way of finding favor. Out on the terrace she would whirl her belt and yell her catchphrase, making branches shiver, birds take flight, clouds drift by. She would clench her teeth and narrow her eyes to slits. Her mother and her friends watching from the veranda were highly amused. Down with men, she could hear them think while they held up their playing cards. None of them had been particularly lucky in love. What they had in common was disillusionment. What they themselves lacked they begrudged others. Their bond did not strike Oda as friendship. It was victimhood, and in order to preserve that bond they guarded each other's misery. They killed time with bridge, glossy magazines, and charitable works. When the women patted Oda on the head, they did so in the belief that the girl was like them. She didn't want their solidarity. She didn't want to be one of them. She was different.

Yes, she had girlfriends, but she kept them at a distance. A phone call when she had something to say, then she could hang up again. None of that scrutiny and interference. No smiles under inquisitive looks. Friendship to her was what she observed between her brothers and their friends. It was a kind of deep-down loyalty that was beyond her. She envied them their camaraderie, in which there was no room for judgmental talk. Her brothers had left home quite young. Their friends stopped coming to the house, her father kept to himself in his attic den. "Down with men," she said over and over again. Only a man with armor would be able to withstand her whip. Paul seemed to be the right man for her. The roles were clearly divided. He laughed at her bad temper, but he was laughing from a distance. He reserved his friendship for his army buddies. He gave her space, but it was not space she was after. She wanted to be pressed back into a mold, the mold of the woman she would have liked to have been but could never be because such women somehow did not exist: straightforward, in control of their lives, and contented. Women are ragged at the edges, they are not clearly defined, their existence is merely an accessory. She envies from the bottom of her heart any woman who denies this and means what she says.

IT'S THE MIDDLE OF THE NIGHT and she's in a strange house in a strange country sitting on a strange toilet, peering through the venetian blinds at the darkness while she pees. She doesn't flush the toilet because she doesn't want to disturb Paul and Oda, just as they, too, didn't flush so as not to disturb her. Their respective waters would blend, how about that for family feeling–her elders shutting the door behind them and then flush, flush, down the drain. She wondered about the guy she'd seen in town this afternoon, the one in the leather jacket with the Judas Priest logo–had he been able to tell that she was a bat? He'd nodded shyly and walked on, a few paces behind his mother. She'd looked around, but he hadn't. She'd thought, *Heaven can wait, I'll be here till the end of time.* She can be such a softy sometimes. Oda and Paul's bedroom door is open, their faces are turned to each other, the wooden crucifix floats over their heads, she's free to do as she pleases. She goes downstairs, seats herself at Oda's desk, and stares at the embroidered motto, at the picture of Vera, at the silver rabbit.

She feels sad about the girl losing her life and the rabbit losing its ear, but she feels even sadder about the woman counting her blessings, for she knows she herself is among them. She remembers Oda's happy smile when she was paying for her new jeans, sweater, and running shoes. They'd strolled through town arm in arm, and when they were sitting side by side at the hairdressing salon Oda had winked at her in the mirror. Later on she'd asked in a confidential tone what sort of boys she liked and she'd described Judas Priest while he was in full view standing in the corner of the lingerie department holding on to his mother's handbag. She didn't dare mention that she'd gone up to him while Oda was busy with the cashier, and that he'd offered to take her for a ride on his motorcycle next week. She walks through to the kitchen. The table's laid for her and Paul with an apple and a fruit knife next to the plates, as if they'll both sit there again in the morning–does death never strike in the night? Oda's breakfast tray is ready by the sink, the coffeemaker has been filled, oranges are waiting by the press. How odd to be doing all these things in advance just to feel time has been saved the next morning. It's pitch-dark outdoors, the animals have all gone to sleep–not the bats, though, but the birds are definitely asleep, and the rabbits probably are, too. She puts on her shoes and a coat, snatches a pack of cigarettes and a lighter from Oda's desk in passing. She opens the kitchen door and steps outside, heads across the lawn and through the bushes, crawls through the hole in the fence. As she nears the charred ruin of the house, the bulldozers loom like alien monsters; she lights a cigarette and sits down by the pool. On the night of the fire she'd felt as if her new life had got off to a grand start, and like then she can see the light burning in the little red bedroom, the window like a cage suspended in the dark.

DAISY'S CLOTHES ARE SCATTERED all over the bed. Oda sniffs at them and lays them carefully across the chair. A cigarette is burning in an ashtray on the floor. She takes a puff and stubs it out. Daisy is in the bath. Singing and splashing. On her pillow are a notebook and a pen. Oda leans over and, without touching the paper, reads: "I don't care if it's a sad goodbye or a bad goodbye, but when I leave a place I like to *know* I'm leaving it." Oda hears the car in the drive. Keys turning in the lock. The front door opening. Oda slips back to her bedroom and gets into bed. Paul comes upstairs. He stands at the foot of the bed in his army gear. Announces: "I got the car back safe and sound."

"Didn't you sleep at all?"

"Only the tough guys stayed up." Paul sits down next to her on the edge of the bed.

"How many of you stayed up?"

"Only Schepers and me."

"What about Emil?"

"He went to bed early."

"How is he?"

"He didn't say much."

"Is he on his own?"

"What do you mean?"

"I mean does he have somebody."

"A woman, you mean?"

"Yes, is that such a crazy question?"

"I don't know, Oda, we didn't discuss women."

Paul gets up and walks to the bathroom. He comes back grumbling: "Can't she shut the door behind her?" and sinks onto the bed. "Emil hardly spoke to me at all. And I haven't seen him in three years! He didn't even drink with the rest of us. And he didn't sleep in the dormitory, he'd booked a room in the officers' hotel."

"You always say buddies don't need to be friends."

"But he *is* a friend, isn't he?"

An earsplitting noise blasts from Daisy's room. Guitar riffs, raw, shrill, delirious, Armageddon. Paul buries his face in her shoulder. "Can't it stop?" he whispers. Oda's thoughts flit anxiously and excitedly to the man whose only wish was to sleep.

TODAY THEY PARK THE CAR ON THE other side of the river and cross to town on the little ferry. The embankment is thronged with parents and children. Oda and Daisy follow the direction of the crowd until they reach the quay. Oda puts on her sunglasses and draws nervously on her cigarette. Santa's steamship looms into view from under the bridge. On the foredeck the figure with the red bishop's miter and the crook, silhouetted against the early sun. As though emerging from the sunlight. The ship is moored and Santa Claus disembarks, followed by his attendants. He makes his way through the mass of children toward the white villa across the street. Parents and children jostle by the fence. Standing on their toes Oda and Daisy catch a glimpse of Santa sitting in the conservatory. Drinking a cup of tea.

"Do you come here every year to see Santa's ship arrive?" asks Daisy.

"I haven't been since Vera died," answers Oda.

They stroll arm in arm through busy shopping streets decorated with bunting and Christmas lights. Happy songs blast from loudspeakers. An organ-grinder plays a tune. In a downtown café they drink hot chocolate. Through the window they watch Santa Claus riding past on his steed, followed by a swarm of excited children. Oda orders a Dutch gin and takes Daisy's hands in hers. "There's so much I still want to tell you," she says. "But then, we've got all the time in the world."

It's quicker to tell the story of a fifteen-year-old than of a fifty-year-old, Daisy muses. So what exactly does it mean: all the time in the world? I can't for the life of me imagine having all the time in world, and besides, it's not even true. Oda's a middle-aged woman and middle-aged women simply don't have that much time left. I'll be going away soon, anyway. So between the two of us we certainly don't have all the time in the world. But I can't see how I can raise that subject just now.

"We don't have much time," Daisy says.

Oda gives her a startled look.

"Even if we had lots of time, it wouldn't be enough," Daisy concludes reassuringly.

INEZ IS STANDING ON THE DOORSTEP. She is wearing a two-piece suit. Her Mini Cooper is parked in the drive. She has come to tell Oda the good news–they have found a new house. Oda thinks, She's come to fetch Daisy. She says, "Oh, that's nice."

Inez says, "It's rather a fancy place, we're going to rent it for a year. We can move in before Christmas. In the meantime we're going to rebuild the old house."

"Is there enough of it left?"

"We're using the foundation. It's going to be a sort of cube. I'll show you the sketches if you like. The old house was such a family sort of place–too much so, really."

"A family sort of place?"

"I mean for kids and family get-togethers, things like that."

"I'd like to see the design sometime," Oda says, holding on to the doorknob.

"The place we've found for now is wonderful. It doesn't have a pool, but there's a sauna. Is Daisy in?" she asks.

"She's gone to town."

"And Paul?"

"I don't know where he is."

"Would you ask Daisy to give me a call?"

"Of course I will," Oda says. She shuts the door.

How dare Inez even consider taking the girl away.

Daisy is all she has. She will guard her like a mother goose, striking great blows with her wings if necessary.

Another ring at the door.

"Oda, there's something else I wanted to ask. I hope you won't mind."

"What is it?"

"Can she stay with you for another week?"

"What? A week?"

"She's going away with her parents in a week's time."

"I didn't know."

"Are you sure you don't mind if she stays a bit longer?"

"No, Inez, it's no trouble at all."

BROWSING IN THE BOOKCASE PAUL happens upon *The Life Cycle of the Human Male,* a book dating from 1958, with the bookplate belonging to Oda's father on the fly-leaf. His eye is caught by the following table: "0–7 years: Age of Imagination; 7–14 years: Building the Self-image; 14–21 years: Puberty and Adolescence; 21–28 years: Carving the Path of Life; 28–35 years: Assessment and Consolidation of the Chosen Path; 35–42 years: Second Puberty, Disorientation about Career Fulfillment; 42–49 years: Conflict Between Sense of Success and Failure; 49–56 years: Struggle Against Decline; 56–63 years: Resignation; 63–70 years: Second Childhood, Acknowledgment of Transition, and Final Resurgence."

. . .

Paul has reached the age of transition between decline and resignation. He has done with the struggle for life, he can start resigning himself. Resigning sounds a bit like dying.

Taking his years of service in the tropics as counting double makes him all of sixty-nine right now, and consequently ripe for a final resurgence. Oda's still in the throes of her struggle against decline. Daisy is about to enter the stage of carving her life's path.

One paragraph has been wholly underlined in red pencil. In the margin a big exclamation mark. It's in the chapter entitled "Senectus." "In this period of seniority one must be fastidious about food, mastication, cleanliness of person and of dress. If these rules are observed, if one does not indulge in idle talk, but saves one's breath for expressing considered opinions, one will earn new affection and respect, and one's advice will be sought." Paul thinks of his father-in-law: locked up by his wife, and no respect from his daughter.

"ODA, WHAT WOULD IT BE LIKE IF we could rewind the past?"

"How do you mean, rewind?"

"Oh, you know, like pushing the rewind button on a cassette recorder."

"Is this a trick question, Daisy?"

"No, it's a riddle."

"I expect you've come up with some idea yourself already."

"I'm asking you."

"Okay, let me think. Well, the dead . . ."

"Gosh."

"The dead could rise from their graves or from their ashes."

"Jesus! And then what?"

"They could grow younger all the time."

"And then?"

"One day they'd be newborn babies."

"Further back, Oda."

"They'd disappear into their mothers."

"Dead."

"Not quite, they'd have another nine months."

"And then?"

"During intercourse the fertilized egg would divide in two, and the sperm cell would shoot back into the father."

"Women would be able to ejaculate."

"I don't know about that."

"What comes next?"

"The woman and the man get younger and younger, too, and eventually end up inside *their* mothers . . ."

"The whole human race would eventually end up inside the very first woman."

"And next to that woman there's a man."

"Adam."

"And the woman vanishes into his rib."

"Oops. How did the story go again?"

"Adam was fashioned out of clay."

"Do you believe that?"

"I once knew someone who believed in a glorious star that exploded at one point. If we could rewind the past, we would, according to that scenario, implode back into the star. A glorious oneness."

"What if you go back even further?"

"You can't."

"Just a teeny-weeny bit."

"I can't go back any further, Daisy. I'm exhausted from all this thinking. We could end up with God, I suppose."

"So God exists!"

"I didn't say that."

"Don't you believe in God?"

"I don't know. I don't ask myself that question anymore."

"How can you not ask yourself that question?"

"You grow out of it. It makes no difference whether he exists or not."

PAUL IS IN THE SHED TINKERING with his damned motorcycle. She had always thought he would never touch it again. Just look at him, on his knees in his outsize pale gray pants, fiddling around with spanners and wrenches. Is he actually taking the whole engine apart? Whenever she had suggested selling the thing because it took up so much space he had refused, saying he wanted to keep it "for later on," as though he had it all planned. Not for a moment had he thought later on might turn out to be completely different.

There's Daisy. Putting her hand on his shoulder while he explains what he's doing. She sinks down on her haunches and listens. An audience for him at last.

He holds the motorcycle steady while Daisy climbs onto the saddle. She grips the handlebars and makes noises like an Indian brave on horseback. She tosses her hair wildly. Paul points at the speedometer. He's having a great time.

The idea that he would have to roam in solitude breaks Oda's heart.

DAISY AND ODA ARE STANDING IN front of the white house where Santa Claus had tea the day before yesterday. Oda has something to deliver, she says. She seems very nervous, pushing up her sunglasses all the time. She rings the bell. No one comes to the door. "Let's go around to the back," she suggests. In the conservatory they find an elderly gentleman in a rattan chair, staring into the distance. Catching sight of them he rises and opens the sliding glass door to let them in. He's tall and thin, wearing a dressing gown and slippers. His eyes have a predatory gleam. Oda introduces her to him. He's the general. He asks Daisy how old she is. Not a polite question to ask a young woman. She doesn't like the way he looks at her and wants him to take his hand off her shoulder. Why doesn't he pay attention to Oda, perched on the sofa still wearing her coat? On a side table the same photograph of Vera as the one in Oda's study. She doesn't like dead people in frames. She doesn't like time standing still. The silence between Emil and Oda is more than she can bear. She takes the binoculars from the windowsill and gazes out over the river. On the ferry she can make out a father holding a baby in his arms, a little flag fluttering behind him. A dog poking its head through the railing. She can hear the silence between Oda and Emil. She's got to get out of here.

Daisy strolls down the quayside toward the old tower. Not that she particularly wants to go for a walk, nor to take another look at the tower, for that matter, she just doesn't want to be with Oda and the general. It really gets to her sometimes, all these old folks making a fuss over nothing. It's freezing. The wind cuts through her wool hat and gloves. She buys a ticket to go to the top of the tower. She doesn't really like climbing. Probably because her parents climb everything in sight. They ruin every vacation with their insistence on going to the top of every mountain or tower they come across, otherwise they feel they've missed something. They can't stand the idea of missing anything at all in their lives. They always make her climb with them. What they're after is for her to have a good time for them.

She starts climbing, counting the steps as she goes. She peers out of the narrow embrasures on the way up. Going round and round the spiral staircase makes her dizzy. She's afraid she might be sick again. Halfway up she stops, sinks down on a step, and puts her head between her knees. She begins to cry and doesn't know why. She feels utterly miserable, loses track of how long she's been sitting there. Half an hour? An hour? There are no other visitors; the place is deserted. Her butt is frozen solid.

In a café at the foot of the tower she orders a Coke. The waitress brings her a minute tumbler. Europeans always act as if it's Chardonnay or something. After smoking four cigarettes one after the other she heads back to the general's house. He gives her a bar of chocolate. They say goodbye. Oda takes a rolled-up drawing out of her bag and offers it to Emil. She says, "For you, from Vera."

In the car on the way home, Oda gives her a hug. She says she could never have done this without her. Next she asks her not to mention their visit to Paul. Daisy promises not to say a word. Her parents never have secrets from each other. Or they don't share them with her. They look with the same pair of eyes and speak with the same mouth. It's not fair. All they want is to be in control. The way they forced this trip on her! They had even told her the news in unison.

Hiding in her tree house she'd overheard her mother talking to her father as she walked him to his car. What she'd said was: "Is it abnormal not to love your own daughter more than anything else in the world?" You don't ever forget words like that.

"Paul, I feel like going to town," Daisy whispers. She's wearing Oda's perfume.

"I'll drive you there," he says, getting up from the bed.

"I'd rather bike."

"I'll take you."

"But you've been drinking." Daisy turns and leaves the room. Paul puts on his bathrobe and slippers and follows her downstairs.

"I'm going to town," she tells Oda, who is lying on the sofa watching television.

"What time is it?" Oda asks.

"Nine o'clock," Daisy mumbles.

"A perfectly normal time for a fifteen-year-old to want to go out," Paul remarks.

"Paul will give you a lift," Oda says, sitting up.

"I'd rather bike."

"Then Paul will ride with you on his bike."

"I'd rather go alone," Daisy says.

Oda gives Paul an accusing look.

"Don't blame me," he says.

Daisy puts on her coat. Paul and Oda walk her to the shed.

"Aren't you cold?" Oda asks. "Where are the gloves and wool hat I got you?"

"I don't need them."

Paul takes out his wallet and slips her a twenty-five-guilder bill. She accepts it with a smile. He checks the tires of her bicycle and decides that the back one needs pumping up. Daisy mounts the bicycle and sets off. Oda and Paul follow her with their eyes until she disappears around the corner. They go back inside together. Oda asks him to come and sit with her. She lays her head in his lap.

"Will you protect me?"

"Of course I will, love."

"And will you forgive me?"

"There's nothing to forgive," he whispers in her ear, "you didn't do anything wrong."

OTTO SPOTTED HER BY THE CIGARETTE machine with her bicycle. She waved at him and beckoned. He knew what she wanted: no one keeps small change in their pockets nowadays. He doesn't normally open the shop for anyone after closing time but decided to make an exception for her, she's a nice girl, always friendly when she comes into the shop, as if she knows. He held the door open and asked if she needed any help. She needed change for twenty-five guilders. He said, "Why don't you step inside for a moment?" She followed him into the shop and through to the back. While he was getting her change, she sat on the couch with her coat on. He asked, "Would you like a drink?" She said that she wasn't thirsty. Did the parrot talk at all, she asked. He said it didn't. She said she didn't like it when parrots talked, it was unnatural. She asked if he ever let it out of its cage, and he replied that he did, now and then. He opened the little door and Jacob perched on the edge. She bent over to inspect the bird, and while she did so, Otto stared at her pretty little rear protruding from her short winter coat. How old would she be? Seventeen, eighteen maybe. Hard to tell with girls these days. She asked, "Do you live alone?" He said that he was married and that his wife was upstairs. She asked if she was already asleep. He said she'd been sleeping for years, she woke up from time to time and then went right back to sleep. She was an invalid. She said that was tough luck. Which was very nice of her, because most of his customers just felt sorry for his wife, while it was worse for him than for her, what with him having sleepless nights with all the worrying. She asked what was wrong with his wife. He said it was hard to explain. He would take her up so she could see for herself. They went upstairs together. He followed behind, eyeing her long legs, her lovely bottom in her jeans. They stood by the bed. She went to sit on the chair next to the bed and looked at his wife. While he stood behind her he wondered whether she would mind if he put his hands on her shoulders. He thought she wouldn't. Perhaps she wouldn't mind if his hands slipped down a bit, either. He couldn't resist and put his hand on her shoulder. She spun around, jumped up from the chair, and said they should be getting back to the parrot. He followed her downstairs. Jacob had returned to his cage. She said she was on her way to town. He offered to accompany her. "You must stay here with your wife," she said. He said he wanted to tell her something. She said, "Go ahead." He asked her not to think badly of him. She said, "Of course not." He said, "I think you're beautiful." She looked at Jacob and then at him.

There was pity in her eyes. Then she said she had a date. "At this hour?" he burst out. "Well, he's a big boy," she answered, smiling.

PAUL COULD TAKE DAISY FOR A REAL trip on his motorcycle. Fix up his machine. Buy a lightweight tent and camp beds, down sleeping bags, a little stove, kitchen equipment. Take the boat. Disembark in New York. Do some sightseeing. Chinatown, Broadway, the city. And then—off they'd go. First to Albany and Syracuse and over the hills, past all the lovely lakes to Niagara Falls. They'd take the cable car and look down on the biggest whirlpools on earth. And at night they'd ride over Rainbow Bridge to the Canadian side to admire the wonderfully illuminated falls. She'd love it! Then they'd ride across southern Ontario. Past Brantford, London, Chatham to the Canadian border at Windsor. They'd take the underwater tunnel to Detroit and be in the United States before midnight. They'd find a little motel and sleep late the next morning. Then on to Chicago. The last leg, from the Illinois state line to Chicago, would offer splendid views across Lake Michigan. Chicago, city of enchantment. The skyline seen from along the lake took your breath away. They'd spend the night at the Hilton in one of its thousand rooms. He'd try to find the clubs he'd been to all those years ago. During the fifties, the Chicago police used to ride Harleys with sidecars. They'd head west on U.S. 20 to Dubuque in Iowa on the Mississippi River. Hills, narrow roads winding through grassland and construction sites. At Dubuque the time difference with New York is one hour. They'd go west again and reach Sioux City on the Missouri River at the Nebraska state line. He'd show her the monument to War Eagle, the great Sioux chief. And then they'd enter South Dakota. The weather would be warming up there. The engine would sweat oil and their lips would become parched in the sun. They'd get a healthy tan. And then to the prairie! They'd ride to Mitchell in the James River valley. He'd show her the Corn Palace, the Oriental palace decorated with corn in Indian patterns, so pretty, she'd think it was fabulous. They'd ride farther and farther west. To the land of cowboys and Indians! The heat would be unbearable and the nights would bring no respite. And then on to Badlands National Park, where the soil erosion was so bad that nothing was left, just a stony wilderness without life. The road across the Badlands snaked through weirdly shaped yellow ravines, where she'd make out castles and cathedrals. At Black Hills they'd leave the prairie behind for good. The temperature would drop and in the distance they'd see the eternal snow on the peaks. Then they'd ride on to Mount Rushmore and the shrine of democracy, where the slopes were wooded with dark green firs and the four American heroes held their heads high. They'd ride through Wyoming, land of high plateaus and mountains—a great ride, rising and falling, changing gears, speeding up and slowing down. They'd round one hairpin bend after another until they reached the mountain pass at the very top, after which they'd begin the descent into the sunset. He recalled the red Rockies, angular and massive, blazing fantastically in the setting sun. The gigantic stone formations would make them feel tiny and insignificant. There'd be the occasional deer and rabbit dashing across the road, they'd even see a bear or two. They'd be welcomed by the rush of little waterfalls as they approached Bighorn National Forest. She'd say she'd never seen such a wonderful sight before, that she'd never been so amazed and filled with awe, and as the moon was so bright and the stars twinkled encouragingly, he'd stop there and pitch the little tent for them to sleep in.

WHERE CAN DAISY BE? HOW COULD they have let her go off on her own like that–a fifteen-year-old girl on a bicycle? She had to cycle past the barracks, the factory buildings, the Gypsy camp, the prostitutes . . . fifteen-year-old girls ought to be in bed by now, Daisy's reckless, she gets out of hand, she's impulsive. What if she . . .

Stop! Gray!

Paul is asleep. He has postponed his preoccupations. Tomorrow is another day, another fresh start, but by then yesterday will be long gone–he is forever escaping. When she met him she thought he had a talent for happiness. She thought he would be a good father to his children. She thought his attitude toward life had to do with wisdom.

. . .

SHE PRESSES HER FACE AGAINST his leather jacket, clasps her hands around his waist, his long hair streams above her head, it's freezing cold, she should've buttoned up her coat but she's such a vain thing, she wanted him to see her unicorn shirt and ask what sort of animal it was so that she could launch into a fascinating conversation about prehistory or something, or about her so-called boyfriend in Orlando. They race through town, across the bridge, along the river and the meadows, over winding roads, this is the highway to hell, it feels great to be so close to him while the world flies past, they go faster and faster, she wants to soar up over the treetops into the darkness of the night, she screams bloody murder at the top of her lungs, they're bats right out of hell, flapping their wings. Beyond the poplar trees the Styx, on the far bank in the real world the illuminated tower, the villa where the general lives. Judas brakes, parks his motorcycle on the shoulder. "Come on," he says, and she follows him across the field to a little shed. He kicks the door open, it smells of clayish soil and grass, she knew it all along, they've outgrown pleasure trips without ulterior motives. He stands facing her, a little awkwardly. They could make a fire, talk about the end of the world, smoke some grass. He reaches out to her, pushes her coat aside, pulls up her shirt, runs cold fingertips over her stomach, her ribs, her new bra, and slides his hands underneath—"You looked so cute holding your mother's handbag," she says teasingly. Judas Priest is not amused. With an earnest look on his face he bends his knees, opens her zipper, and strips down her jeans, then slips his hand into her panties and runs his fingers between her thighs. His face is up close, she feels his hands all over her midriff and her breasts, she throws her head back, his long hair tickles her, his tongue drives her crazy. Judas tears off his jacket, spreads it on the ground, she lays her sheepskin coat over it and lies down, he stands at her feet and unzips his pants, lowers himself onto her. "Stop right there!" she yells under her breath, and she grits her teeth, for she must surrender. She can hear Ellen Foley singing inside her head about love and need and fidelity, but she doesn't particularly care if this Meatloaf says yes or no. Gazing into his dark eyes she can feel him probing into her. This is the sixth time in her life, one day she'll have done it so often that she'll have lost count. He tries to kiss her, but she won't let him, she's thinking of Paul and Oda, perhaps they're worried sick, they don't want anything to happen to her. While Judas thrusts and groans on top of her she has the feeling someone's watching, spying on them from a point just above Judas's head, a ferocious, damning look. I can tell you're there, she thinks, and do you know how I can tell? You know what I mean. I'm talking about being able to see without using your eyes. Panting heavily, Judas comes—on her stomach, thank goodness. She wipes off her stomach with the inside of her shirt, pulls her jeans on, scrambles to her feet, buttons her coat tight, and turns up the collar. "Let's go," he mumbles.

They climb onto the motorcycle and ride back to town. She's so cold, if only she'd had the sense to take her wool hat and gloves. She wonders how long it'll take her to get home from the café where she left her bike. Judas drops her off in front of the café. He has to get home on time. He shakes her hand and rides off in his cool Judas Priest jacket, back to Mom, of course. It probably wasn't even a proper motorcycle, just a souped-up moped. And the foxtail dangling from the saddle was unbelievably pathetic.

A BICYCLE ON THE DRIVE. PAUL wakes up. The dynamo whirring against the front tire. Oda swears as she gets out of bed. She slips her dressing gown on and goes downstairs. Paul follows her down to the hall. She goes into the kitchen. He hears a dull thud, a shout. Then all is quiet.

He calls out, "Oda!"

No reply.

He calls again, "Daisy!"

No reply.

He sits down on the bottom step of the staircase. He doesn't dare go in and look. He knows that as soon as he sticks his head around the kitchen door he will have to avert his eyes. He looks up at the alligator on the hat rack, its goggle eyes staring blankly. He can hear Daisy whimpering, Oda sobbing. Paul gets up and walks to the kitchen. The two women are weeping in each other's arms.

· · ·

SHE DIDN'T WANT THIS, BUT SHE couldn't help herself. Daisy turns away. Oda wants to take her words back, but it's too late for that now. Daisy shakes her off, she frees herself from her hold, but says nothing. Oda looks at Paul raising his hand to his throat, she can't stand this, it isn't like her at all, she loves Daisy. How can she ever make amends, she's beside herself, she feels all black inside, rotten, she can't do anything right, her whole life seems a downward spiral to this terrible moment, for she knows how it will turn out. Daisy will go away. Their chances are ruined, she has broken the rules, she is out of the game, has shown what she is capable of, and what one is capable of is one's true nature. She is guilty, and no one will understand. Paul leans over to her. He will console her, tell her he understands, but how can he understand if she herself doesn't understand. She can't abide his hand on her shoulder, she doesn't want to hear his gentle soothing voice. "I love you," he whispers with tears in his eyes, but she doesn't want his love, she isn't worth it. "Go away," she whispers. He looks at her wretchedly, takes his hand off her shoulder, and follows Daisy up the stairs.

THE NEXT EVENING. THE RAIN LASHES against the windowpane, the wind whistles around the house. The sound of the television is carried upstairs through the central heating pipes, Daisy's playing music in her room. He hears footsteps heading to the bathroom, a steady stream lasting twenty seconds and ending abruptly, the lashing rain, the gurgle of the television, footsteps on the landing, a knock on the door. It's Daisy. In a low voice she says, "Please come and tuck me in," and Paul follows her to her room. She gets into bed and lies on her back, smiling at him. He covers her with the duvet and sits down beside her. She says it was all her fault. He says it wasn't. She lifts up the duvet and says, "Come and lie down for a moment." Paul hesitates. She lays her hand on the nape of his neck and draws him close; he slumps onto the bed with his back to her, pulls up his knees, feels her covering him with the duvet, feels her body against his while his eyes slide from the little red desk to the purple plastic container with the hanging plant and then to the pattern on the curtains. He wants to move away but she won't let him, he can hear the lashing rain, the whistling wind. He sits bolt upright. "I've got to go," he says, but Daisy pulls him back. He says, "What if Oda sees us," but Daisy says, "Oda's not here to see." He says she's likely to barge in without knocking, but Daisy says, "No way." She climbs over him, goes to the door, and turns the key, comes back to bed and asks, "Don't you ever feel lonely?" He doesn't answer, he feels her legs sliding along his legs, her hands running down his arms to his belly, her knees nudging the backs of his knees, her little feather earrings tickling his neck. "I love you," she whispers, he says she doesn't know what she's saying, she whispers, "I think I love you." He says he loves her, too, the way a father loves his daughter, and his thoughts go to her father, who's probably thinking of her at this very moment, thinking lovingly of her, but

117

then perhaps she doesn't really have a father, nor a mother for that matter, perhaps it's all made up and she's all alone in the world, because no girl would appear suddenly out of a sea of flames unless she were all alone in the world. He tries to loosen her grip but she says, "No, you're staying here." He twists his head around to look at her. "So you'll stay," she says, and through the thin fabric of her T-shirt he can feel her bare skin. "You're like a little Oda," he tells her. "I'm not a little Oda," she splutters, "I'm a bat out of hell." Paul laughs and she tries to kiss him but he averts his face. He's trying his utmost to think, his inner voice yells, "This is all wrong, I can't do this," and he listens to Oda's heels tapping downstairs, to the patter of the rain, the thumping of the girl's heart. "You need me," she whispers, and he thinks of drowning and wrestling while the thumping grows louder, becomes pounding, their two hearts beating as one, the two of them in the chamber of a single heart, together in Vera's room, in Vera's heart, and he thinks, She'll be gone soon and she'll be gone forever, and this is the last chance he'll ever get as long as he lives.

PAUL LIFTS DAISY'S HEAVY SUITCASE into the trunk. Oda sees Daisy glance up at the house. She has promised to come back in a couple of weeks, but Oda knows the way people look when they are saying goodbye forever. Oda slides behind the wheel, leaves the door open. Daisy gets in beside her and lets out a sigh while she tosses her hair back, a sigh of relief. Oda eases the car down the driveway with Paul walking abreast of them as far as the border stones. Daisy chatters excitedly about Paris. Her parents will be meeting her train tonight at the Gare du Nord. They will marvel at the beauty and splendor of the jewel in the old crown of Europe, they will delight in being reunited as a family . . . As they drive past the stationery shop Daisy's face has a look of finality, and her look is the same when they go past the Juliana Hotel, the church, the cemetery. They drive through the backstreets of town with the prostitutes, they go under the bridge and along the embankment, the sun low in the sky making the river glisten and the ferry burst through the glitter. When they go past Emil's house, Daisy leans forward and peers at the windows. "Will you give him my love?" she asks with a smile. Daisy has no idea. Oda makes a right turn and pulls up in front of the train station. She looks at Daisy's pretty profile, the eyes staring ahead, the body about to absent itself from her for good. Seeing the river disappear in the rearview mirror she feels as though she is losing a daughter all over again.

SHE WATCHED ODA WAVE GOODBYE, she watched her waving and receding as if she were rubbing herself out of Daisy's life, she watched the station dwindle and vanish, the trees in the park, then the river, the general's house, the tower she didn't dare go up all the way, the bridge under which she'd seen Santa Claus loom into view. Holding her head out of the window, her hair swathed across the water like a soft paintbrush dipped in a thousand colors. She felt a tap on her shoulder: it was an old lady asking her to shut the window. She did and settled into her seat. Swallowing was painful, and she squirted half the contents of the camomile spray Oda had given her into the back of her throat. In her bag she found a small foil-wrapped package containing a cheese and tomato sandwich: Oda's last maternal deed. Her spirits sank as she tried to imagine Paul and Oda having to get on with their lives without her, she had the feeling she'd stolen something from them. What would they look like in five years, or ten, would they still be alive, would they still be together, and what would she herself look like? What sort of a person would she have become when they were long dead and gone? She was nearly sixteen, she'd be an adult soon, and she'd have other things on her mind.

She looks at the face of the passenger sitting across from her, sees the old lady's eyes darting back and forth as if she doesn't want to miss the slightest detail of the world flying past . . . The train slows down and comes to a squeaking halt in the middle of meadows with grazing cattle. The old lady smiles at her and says, "Perhaps there's a rabbit on the track."

Daisy giggles. Fantastic that someone so old should make such a comic remark.

"What's so funny?" the old lady asks suspiciously.

"The rabbit," Daisy says. She pictures a rabbit sitting up on the rail with an admonishing front paw saying, "Stop!"

The old lady unfolds her newspaper and begins to read. The light falling through her crochet hat makes little flecks on her face. Like shiny granules, she thinks. If I blow on them her whole face'll change, the granules will resettle into different combinations, she'll be a different person. Daisy looks at the whole world in this way sometimes: gleaming granules forming ever-changing patterns, faces turning into other faces, towns into other towns, landscapes into other landscapes, and when she focuses this notion on herself, it's just as if she, too, is transformed.

It has started to rain, the granules turn into drops, fat raindrops on the windowpane flowing together to form the inky ruins of Hans and Inez's house, dark rivulets breaking loose and spreading across the garden, the rabbit making a dash for its burrow, the foxtail flying from Judas's saddle drawing a little stippled line . . . the train gathers speed . . . a ship, a submarine, droplets creeping upward, tremulously shaping a jellyfish, a ghost, a creature from outer space.

The old lady puts down her newspaper and stares outside again, her small eyes don't want to miss a thing.

WHEN DAISY'S TRAIN HAS LEFT, ODA walks back to her car. The first Christmas trees are being sold on the sidewalk. A couple of teenage girls are smoking cigarettes and giggling in the sunlight. Oda's thoughts are of death. Her own death. It was on just such a day as this that the biology teacher drove to the tower block behind the school, took the elevator to the eleventh floor, walked down the gallery clutching her handbag, and flung herself over the railing. Oda often thinks of her. She pictures her lying there. She always wore such smart boots. She sees her lying there with those boots and the matching leather handbag. The splattered body. Oda tells herself not to be silly. She is not the kind of woman who jumps to her death. She gets into her car, slides the sunroof open, and lights up. She drives to the center of town. Parks the car behind the supermarket, and walks to the fish market, which is full of women with their winter coats hanging open. Mothers with sons and daughters shopping for Christmas. She asks for a pair of filleted sole. She will be home soon, she will cook for Paul and herself and then lie on her stomach watching television. She intends to go back to her car but heads in the opposite direction. Toward the tower and the river. They're putting up Christmas decorations at the restaurant. Children on a school outing throng the entrance to the tower, their eyes fixed anxiously on the top.

Oda was one of the mothers accompanying the excursion the year that Vera's class visited the tower. Her little girl had been so frightened. It had been Oda's idea to go along. Vera didn't want to go up to the top, but she had to. It was only later that Oda realized that Vera had thought she would have to climb the tower the way you climb a mountain, on the outside, with nothing but ropes and picks for support. The teacher hadn't told her about the steps inside the tower going all the way to the top. Oda had been so relieved to see that Vera was relieved, and she thought she was so brave, stepping right ahead and up all those steps. Her beloved little girl. They had stood on the top together. Dozens of children gazing out over the town, peering over the balustrade. Oda looked at the fast-flowing river and at Emil's house. She put her hands on Vera's little shoulders. She felt vulnerable. The sky was so near, the earth so far. Vera had asked, "Are you scared?" The bells had started ringing.

Losing a daughter. A daughter whose shouts, cries, peals of laughter, whether near or far, were like birdsong in the woods, a voice marking boundaries and giving definition to her world. Ever since that voice fell silent Oda's world has lacked definition.

She walks to the river with her fish fillets, then turns right. The old city gate is flanked by agaves. She should not be doing this. She walks on, past the gables flooded with sunlight, the lime trees with their glossy branches. Cows and horses in the fields across the river. She puts her hand on the garden gate. In the conservatory she can see the top of Emil's head. She goes up the path and knocks on the window. Emil jumps up and lets her in. As if he has been waiting for her. He glances at the parcel she is carrying and asks what she's got there. "Fillets of sole for two," she says, smiling. She goes up the stairs, runs into the bedroom, and falls on the bed. The gold baton gleams in the corner of the room. Emil sits down beside her, she stretches out. Neither of them speak. Through the windows she sees a flock of birds flying past. She hears a train thundering over the bridge. A ray of light catches on Emil's funny protruding ears, making them luminous. The hairs on his chest have turned gray. He regards her with surprise. No doubt she, too, has changed. He takes her in his arms and presses his lips to hers, she pulls him close, lays her head on his old man's belly. Her body lets go of her mind. It has started to rain. She dozes off. The sleep of homecoming. How long she lies there she does not know. She gets up from the bed and crosses to the bathroom. She strokes her silk dressing gown with her fingers.

PART 4

1987

ONE

*E*mil is standing on the riverbank. He stares into the gray water. Circles and streaks. Six kilometers an hour. March time. What day is it, no idea, what month, he breaks into a sweat, is it spring or autumn, the sun hangs low over the river, dazzles him, where is he, he glances around, all gone, blank, empty, this kind of thing is liable to happen to people his age, they just drop dead because they don't know where they are, who they are, what is top and what is bottom, it's all over, this must be the afterlife. Suddenly he sees her. She welcomes him. The horizon floats a little above her knees. The sand all around is covered in her small footprints. The long brown hair is brushed to one side. The right hand holds the hair against the neck, the other hand rests on the left leg. She hunches her shoulders. Draws in her stomach, making a shadow around the navel.

Her face is pale, her look at once wary and yearning, perhaps because she hasn't yet turned out the way she wants. The mouth is small, slightly peevish. For a moment she stands in the full glare. The water behind her and the sand at her feet recede. She melts into the air. Emil tries to banish her from his thoughts, but the sheer effort makes him think of nothing else. What is the weight of time if memories do not fade and desire does not wane?

A few gulls, a Rhine barge. Across the water in the long grass some wild horses, bison, cows. A small nature reserve. Prehistoric times. On the left by the bridge the windmill. At times it seems as if everything—flowing water, ferry, river craft, cars crossing the bridge, people going for walks—is set in motion by that little windmill. Stick a finger between the sails and everything will stop.

Yesterday, having lunch with the widow of a former colleague in a restaurant in Amsterdam, he couldn't take his eyes off a little boy holding a giant egg, the top half of which he kept raising to reveal a dinosaur. Looking at him he imagined that the boy recognized him. Perhaps the child recognized in the elderly gentleman's eyes his own wonderment at the creature inside the egg, a sentiment which he could not share with his young parents. He reminded Emil of someone he had known long ago. A pale, fair-haired lad. A water rat. Paul Klein.

Emil tried to concentrate on his companion's monologue. It was a detailed account of the illnesses suffered by colleagues and colleagues' wives as well as recent deaths, and each time she asked, "Do you remember So-and-so?" Emil would know that that person had died or had suffered a bereavement. In the meantime, he watched the little boy clamping the two halves of his egg together and then pulling them apart to display the ghoulish, scary creature inside. Emil envied him his egg, which he would have liked to hold himself, and envied him the mother's hand reaching out from time to time to touch his cheek, and the father's watchful eyes, but Emil also envied the mother and the father for having a child to whom they were drawn as to a cozy fire in the grate. He raised his eyes to meet those of his companion, whose conversation had petered out. The silence between them was suffused with waiting, with the expectation that he would fill the gaping void left behind by her eulogy of death. But Emil's presence here was sheer happenstance, she must understand that. His motives were practical: this was one of the days when he was entitled to a reduced train fare. So why not go to Amsterdam for the day? If the weather was good he could drink beer in an open-air café and have a bite to eat with a friend, perhaps go for a stroll afterward. By now the widow was looking very miserable indeed. Reeling off the names of the sick and the dead had made her vivacious, but now that she had reached the end of her list she had collapsed like a soufflé. Emil for his part felt vigorous, and asked after her two sisters, one of whom he had flirted with long ago during an army reception at the Zwaluwenberg. The widow sitting opposite him said,

"Stories about old people turn into life stories." You don't say, he thought. Somehow he hadn't quite registered what she was saying. Things escaped him. Maybe that was what they meant by the weight of time. Watching her walk down the canal after saying goodbye he was filled with self-loathing. And he called out, "Odette, Odette," but she did not hear, or did not wish to hear. And he was too much of a coward to go after her. But the worst part was: she wasn't Odette at all.

Emil's mood darkened. He could do with something to raise his spirits. He stepped into the ice-cream parlor and treated himself to a double dip of vanilla. Then he bought a box of praline chocolates. He glanced up at the Royal Palace the way he used to do in the old days with Oda and Vera, and with a stomachache he made his way to the station. On the train home he took a seat with a folding table in the hope that someone would come and sit opposite him, but no one did. He drew a doodle on an old newspaper.

That was how he used to carry Vera on his shoulders. She would be wearing her tartan skirt, would wrap her legs around his neck. She would pull her skirt down over his face so that he couldn't see a thing. He would shout between her legs for her to lift the skirt. She would shriek with delight and keep pulling it down. He used to long for her to be his daughter.

Emil got home at ten o'clock. He took a beer from the fridge and sat down on the sofa. He stared out the window across the dark river. He felt an urge to go out again. An evening stroll. When he reached the church he stopped to look up at the tower. Then he headed toward the bridge. He went past the old city walls and the girls lounging in the doorways of their curtained cubicles. They motioned him to come inside but he walked on. He went up the steps and wandered across the bridge. He stopped in the middle, rested his hands on the railing. In the distance he could see a light burning in his house. It was the toadstool lamp in Vera's room.

TWO

*B*eing dead is like what you are before birth, Emil thought. Ceylon, 1943. He was lying on a beach looking up at the stars. He had stopped believing in heaven, or indeed in the Elysian fields, unlike his best buddy Klein, who had fallen asleep on the sand beside him. Ready to die for queen and country. Klein was convinced that when he died he would go to the fields of honor, like all his pals. Not the wives and children, though. They died and went to heaven. Emil listened to the sound of the sea. Klein was snoring softly, his lips were parted. Emil envied him his carefree, trusting nature.

Stories about old people turn into life stories. The widow's words. Life reduced to facts and milestones. Death as the final curtain. Emil had first set eyes on

Klein at the municipal swimming pool in their home-town. He saw him standing at the water's edge, shudder-ing with fright and excitement. A fair-haired, pale boy, his skin white as milk. Gazing in awe at the swimming instructor, who asked him, "How about joining the Wa-ter Rats?" Klein answered in a tremulous, high voice, "I'll ask my father." Emil stood in the water leaning his shoulders against the side of the pool, staring in fascina-tion at the boy with his frail build, three or four years younger than himself. It was as though Emil had lost his own innocence through observing it in Klein. From that moment on their roles were fixed.

Klein's father said it was all right for him to join the Water Rats. Emil was his monitor. He taught him the basic swimming techniques and how to push off and turn around. He would give a demonstration that Klein would imitate. Klein was very eager, he wanted to go swimming every day. He was hard on himself. He hated it when he could not keep up with Emil. Emil taught him that success is more important than failure, and also that winning doesn't necessarily bring success. The goal must be set high, but it must be attainable. Klein was a faithful puppy, eager for training. At Emil's hands.

Emil did not believe in the field of honor, nor in heaven, only in celestial bodies. At school he had learned about Lemaître, the Belgian scientist who argued that all mat-ter was originally contained in a single primal atom. Bil-lions of years ago this giant atom had exploded, thereby sending particles of matter careening into space. We humans live on a cooled-off cinder, we observe all the suns dying slowly and try to recall the vanished glory of the world's beginning. A firework display that has just ended. The best part is over. Life after the event.

Emil joined the army in the late 1930s. Klein was in his final year at secondary school; he swam, rowed, and tinkered with an old motorcycle. When he was on leave Emil would visit him at the house behind the station where Klein's father ran a printing business, or they would meet at the swimming pool. He had kept up his daily training. Over long distances he outswam Emil. But winning was not his goal. Klein wanted Emil to be proud of him. The war put an end to their meetings. Emil was stationed with his battalion in Zeeland. Fleeing the advancing German forces he crossed to England from Dunkirk on a British vessel. He was unable to maintain contact with Holland. He thought of his young friend with nostalgia. And jealousy. Klein belonged to him.

In 1942 Emil went to Scotland. The Commando Basic Training Center needed fresh recruits. His English colleagues warned him that it was "hell on earth" up there. Emil was ambitious. It was a course for elite soldiers. His arrival in hell was more like a homecoming. As he got off the bus he spotted a young soldier standing on the grass with his hand on his hip and a cigarette in his mouth. Catching sight of Emil the young soldier leapt up in the air like a puppy and ran toward him. It was Klein! Emil hugged him, lifted him up, and swung him around and around. They belonged together.

The training was exhausting. Everything had to be done in doubletime, they almost forgot how to walk at a normal pace. The use of blanks was unheard of, which meant that the maneuvers were carried out under fire of Bren guns and explosives. They learned to shoot with every type of gun from every conceivable position, to hit their target under all circumstances. They practiced unarmed combat and excelled in the use of the commando dagger. They were trained in parachuting, climbing rock faces, driving locomotives, crossing ravines by means of bridges made of toggle ropes. In the middle of all the training in special skills they were sent out on field exercises in remote areas under a steady downpour, and later in the bitter cold of winter. Klein faithfully kept a diary for his father, a few excerpts of which were eventually published in a memorial book in honor of the Select Commando Corps.

Dear Father,
My first trip in the jeep was great. They let me
take the wheel. You should have seen me sitting
in that boxy vehicle. We drove in a convoy
across the Scottish highlands. I was in the
middle and had been instructed to look around
from time to time to check whether the rest
were following okay, just as the occupants of

the other jeeps had to keep an eye on the ones following them. This is the life! Driving a jeep, speeding in a convoy across God's beautiful nature! The valleys! The peaks! On and on. Toward the unknown. I had my hand on the windshield, and I felt as if I could bend the material. That's how strong I felt, how free, how steadfast. Oops, thud: a pothole. And another. A wild cross-country chase. The jeep swerved like a rudderless ship in a storm. All I could do was change gears again and again, wrench the wheel this way and that, and hold on for dear life. And get my wits together so as to keep my legs and rear and back and shoulders and elbows under control, and my eyes on the road as well. Splatters of mud flew around my ears. Yet another series of potholes and ruts. It was like riding a bumper car at a fair. Boing, went the jeep, right through the shock absorbers. The windshield got knocked out of place, not thanks to my firm grip but thanks to my poor head! And my knee got a bad knock. The jeep creaked and rattled and shook and bumped, crash, boom, blub . . . and there I was: stuck.

Klein and Emil made a good team. At the end of the training period they were issued their green berets. Both were promoted: Emil to the rank of first lieutenant and Klein to that of staff sergeant. In the spring they embarked with the Insulinde Corps for Ceylon. From there they were to infiltrate Sumatra for the purpose of gathering information on the Japanese occupiers and locating prisoner-of-war camps. Sitting around the campfire at night drinking whiskey, Klein would talk about animals and motorcycles while Emil thought only of girls and women. One night they were visited by a fortune-teller. She told Klein that he would father one child and that the child would be lost to him. Emil roared with laughter because Klein himself was still a child. The old woman looked accusingly at Emil, either because he was laughing or, it occurred to him years later, because she knew it was he who would one day rob Klein of his child.

THREE

On August 10, 1973, Emil got up at six-thirty, put on his T-shirt, shorts, and running shoes. The weather was misty and warm. He did some stretching exercises at the water's edge and then ran along the quay toward the old footbridge. He mounted the steps, crossed the bridge, and headed down the path skirting the flood-plain. The little ferry cast off from its mooring, a flock of ducks flew across the river, a cow stood knee-deep in the water. The sun broke through the mist. Emil slowed down when he reached the horses. He picked some grass and offered it to them. They eyed him in their usual way, calm and trusting. Behind their swishing tails he could make out his house veiled in the mist. On the way back he took the new railway bridge and concluded his morning run with exercises in the same place as before. Emil had his breakfast and read the paper. He looked out the window and in his mind's eye he could already see his little girl drawing pictures at the garden table, balancing on the edge of the lavender bed, dashing across the lawn with the pear trees, the nut trees, running to who knows where.

Oda arrived at midday. Emil opened the gate and the garage doors. She parked inside and got out of her car. She was wearing her tennis skirt and white polo shirt. Holding Vera's toadstool lamp in her hand. Emil lifted two heavy suitcases out of the trunk and carried them inside. She had already brought some of her belongings here on previous occasions. The silk dressing gown hanging on the bathroom door, for instance, and the bottle of Quadrille perfume, which he sniffed every morning and night.

While he was carrying the suitcases into the house he felt Oda's hand on his shoulder. He put the cases down and allowed her to lead him up the stairs. She pulled him onto the bed with her and clung to him. He kissed her neck, squeezed her calves with his fingers, slipped off her shoes. Oda got down on all fours. She threw him a teasing look, her long hair swinging from side to side. Emil lunged at her. She was strong and agile. She turned Emil on his back and sat on his stomach. She held his arms splayed out on the mattress. "Surrender," she said. "I surrender," sighed Emil. He couldn't get enough of this woman.

Over time she had transformed his home into their home. The old heavy furniture had been replaced by furniture they both liked. Light and cheerful. The kitchen had been modernized and for Vera they had built a separate bathroom next to her bedroom. The house had been painted inside and out. Emil loved to observe his beautiful lover imposing her will on the house. She had taste and determination. The military souvenirs in the hall had been ruthlessly relegated to his study in the attic.

They spent the day decorating Vera's new room. They put down fawn carpeting. They hung new pale blue curtains. Emil assembled the new bed while Oda took Vera's clothes out of the suitcase and arranged them on the empty shelves of the new closet. Now and then she held up a little dress, smiling and saying, Isn't it adorable. Emil said "adorable" was not in a general's dictionary. Oda placed the toadstool lamp on the windowsill. Her little girl wouldn't go to sleep without it. Emil and Oda stood close together by the window, looking out over the river. "I'm going to teach her to sail. I'll get her one of those little sailing dinghies," Emil said. "She's a true-blue Water Rat." Oda hugged him and whispered, "You'll make a wonderful father." She was shocked at her own words.

As the afternoon drew to a close they prepared supper together. Emil fried a trout. Oda made a salad. Emil uncorked a bottle of white wine. Oda laid the table under the nut tree. They sat facing each other quietly, the first moment of rest after a busy day. Emil proposed a toast to

Oda, but she didn't think the moment was right for toasting. She did not look happy. They ate the food on their plates in silence. Oda was facing a daunting task. There was nothing Emil could do to help.

After supper Oda showered and changed her clothes. She came downstairs in a pale beige summer dress. Emil wanted desperately to lift her up and carry her upstairs again, but Oda had to go. She moved out of his arms. Oda backed her car into the road. Emil walked alongside as far as the gate. She stuck her hand out of the open sunroof and sounded the horn. She sped away into the setting sun. Road and river flowed together in a ribbon of gold. Emil was afraid she would never come back.

FOUR

*O*da's obiter dicta. You must try all the combinations until you hit the correct one, shuffle all the options until they fall into place, the kind of place that feels right, that feels like home.

1964. A reception at the Zwaluwenberg with the prince's chiefs of staff. Emil had just returned from his posting in the Caribbean. Klein had recently been promoted to the rank of major. In his arms the most beautiful woman Emil had ever seen. Emil's and Oda's eyes met. Fireworks. Inner, primal bliss. With a shock Emil realized that they belonged together. He knew she felt the same. The presence of his young friend, gazing on his young, pregnant wife with pride and love, did not stop Emil from wanting to have her for himself. The idea that

Klein of all people should turn up with the woman of his dreams . . . Emil and Oda looked at him sadly. He was wreathed in smiles. Sooner or later he would become a casualty of their love. It would not be until many years later, but this love was patient.

Emil recommended his friend for a staff position in his division. Klein was charged with stores and equipment. He was cut out for logistics. An officer of great punctiliousness, he was authoritarian to his subordinates and obedient to his superiors. Discipline, loyalty, duty, those words were more than dear to him, they were sacred, a basic necessity, central to his existence. As though life without discipline, loyalty, and duty were impossible. He was perfectly attuned to his environment, not so much out of an interest in friendship but rather because he was attracted to the team spirit, to the notion of a body of men that was like a well-oiled machine. Maybe a parallel could be drawn here to his relationship with Oda: he would talk about the two of them being a good team, and would say things like "We didn't do too badly, did we?"

Emil was able to share with Odette the kind of thoughts one must keep to oneself because they are not supposed to enter one's mind. Together they spoke a forbidden language. A secret code. It was their conspiracy against the world. They would play Scrabble for hours on end, forming words that did not exist. You could call it love, but Oda didn't like that word. She maintained that love had been invented by people who needed a word for it.

By people like Oda and Paul, for instance. Oda and Emil were different. They were past love. They were one. Love could no longer come between them. Love could not divide them. But they would be divided in the end. Not by love, but by death. Not their own death, but the death of the child. The words that did not exist would be of no use to them then.

To Emil, Vera stood for the future. Her expectation was his expectation. Her world expanded by the day, and Emil's world grew accordingly. Through Vera he saw Oda as a little girl, and through Oda he saw Vera as a grown woman. When he visited Oda and Paul at home, he would go up to Vera's room to tuck her in bed. With a dreamy look in her eyes she would ask him to draw the patterned curtains, switch off the lights in her dollhouse, straighten the row of cuddly toys at the foot of her bed, and please not to go away. She would make him promise to stay forever and ever, cross his heart, and when he had done so, she would lift the covers invitingly. It was beyond comprehension . . . that one time when the distinction between Oda and Vera had eluded him, when his fingers had slid down to her shoulders, had stroked her smooth body, and he had drawn her onto his lap, had pressed his forehead against hers, had kissed her mouth. The borderline had become blurred imperceptibly with each time she stared him down, each time she clamped her short legs around his neck, each time she pulled her little skirt down over his head.

FIVE

Oda returned at eleven o'clock, on foot. She did not have Vera with her. She fell into his arms, sobbing. Emil's first thought was that Klein would not let her go. Of course he wouldn't. No man in his right mind would let her go. But it wasn't anything like that. They got into his car and drove to the mortuary. They sat together at the bedside for a long time, staring at the pinched face with the lips set in an angry line saying NO. They drove back in silence. As they lay on the bed Emil wondered if they could ever be happy now. The answer was no. Their lives would be ridden with guilt. Oda must go back to Klein, there was no other way. Oda whispered that she couldn't, wouldn't, go back. He was adamant. He stuffed her clothes back into the suitcases and carried them to his car. Oda trailed after him, in tears. He drove her home. The sun was rising over the river. The landscape was blue. Emil stopped the car at the border stones. He took the cases out of the trunk and set them down on the curb. Oda kissed him on the mouth. She had to. It was an order. She flexed her knees, curled her delicate fingers around the handles, and lifted the cases. He watched Oda going up the drive. She was unsteady on her feet. He felt himself to be the worst coward the world had ever known.

Emil did not see her again until the funeral. She was standing next to Klein, wearing a black dress. She ignored Emil. With Klein gripping his arm Emil wondered which was worse: the death of a child or the death of love. Worst of all was when the two came together. Klein was convulsed with grief. Emil thought–he was aware that what he was thinking was cruel, but that did not stop him from pursuing this line of thought quite freely and with abandon–that Paul ought to be damn grateful to him for giving him his wife back before he had truly stolen her away.

S I X

A man deprived of love becomes invisible and might just as well be dead. That was how Emil felt ever since Vera died. Life had turned out different than he had expected. He retired from the army. He had a few ladyfriends, but none of them could replace Oda. He did not dare visit Oda at home, feeling that this would be a torment to her as well as to himself. Klein was puzzled by Emil's aloofness and kept trying to persuade him to drop by. Emil had to invent a lot of excuses. He would bump into Klein at army functions like the corps dinners, receptions, commando reunions.

When Klein accepted the offer of a post in Paramaribo, Emil hoped Oda would come back to him. She neither phoned nor visited. He glimpsed her in her car from time to time, and one day he found himself standing behind her at the fish market, but she was studying the shrimps with such concentration that he knew she had no desire to see him.

After Vera died Emil was left with two visions of the future. One imaginary, the other real. One with Oda and Vera, and the other without them. The time when Oda turned up on the doorstep with the teenage girl it was as though dream and reality had switched places. The girl had held back, had been eager to get out of the house. Emil and Oda had stayed behind, together. Oda repeated her reproaches of seven years earlier. He had deserted her at the very time that she needed him most. Emil said he had done it for Klein's sake. "So who was more important," raged Oda, "Paul or me?" Oda did not expect an answer. Emil pointed to the flowers he put in a vase each year to mark her birthday. They were wilting.

The girl returned. It was time for them to go. Oda took a drawing out of her bag and gave it to him. "From Vera for Emil." Emil was speechless. To him the picture of the child approaching the empty house meant a terrible indictment. Oda and the girl walked away arm in arm across the road to the riverbank. When they reached the ferry they turned and waved at him.

Oda showed up again a week later, unaccompanied this time. She took his hand and led him up the stairs. She said jokingly that she had forgotten how it went, but their bodies had not forgotten. In the morning she vanished. Emil had not had the courage to ask when she would come back. She had left a parcel of fish in the kitchen, so he thought, She'll be back soon. He kept the sole fillets for three days. They started to smell bad. He kept them one more day. The smell was overpowering. In the end he threw them out, with tears in his eyes. He decided he was wrong not to have asked Oda when he would see her again. Perhaps it was all a misunderstanding. Since then not a day has gone by without him waiting in the wings, hoping for her to be restored to him. Growing old does not necessarily lower one's expectations. He continued to live his imaginary life with Oda in anticipation of the day when the dream would coincide with reality, a reality that would transform his failed life into a tremor on the horizon.

SEVEN

*R*eunion day at Roosendaal. Blustery weather. Emil and Paul bump into each other in the thick of a gathering attended by several hundred soldiers sporting blazers and green berets. They slap each other on the back. Paul looks well and happy. He says Emil should really drop by sometime and take a look at his young Labrador. Perhaps Emil would like to look after the dog during the summer, when they'll be taking a trip to Indonesia. A long-awaited opportunity to show Oda where he served during the colonial war. Emil feels uneasy. He fears that Klein will notice that he is jealous. The commander in chief summons everyone present to assemble on the parade ground. He asks for a moment's silence to commemorate their fallen comrades. Then the sky brightens. Emil says, "What did I tell you, the Lord looks kindly on us commandos," at which Klein winks and asks if he will be joining the march. Emil shakes his head. He is feeling a bit under the weather. The various divisions align themselves on the field. Klein walks toward the Insulinde Corps. There are only six men left. Emil sees Paul motioning him to come over. He can't very well refuse. The march starts at the soccer field. They advance with three men abreast. Emil is on Klein's left. Now and then Emil glances sideways, he can see that Klein is fully absorbed in his role. Enviably so. He marches in perfect time. Straight-backed, in exemplary fashion, swinging his right arm up to shoulder height and carrying his coat neatly over his left. The silent type. The thoughts in his mind are not only the kind of thoughts Emil can think for himself, they go before, beneath, beyond that. Observing him in this way enables Emil to develop trains of thought that would not have occurred to him otherwise, ideas that are inextricably tied up with Klein. He always wanted to discover how Klein's mind works, that's all, for Klein is his friend, the only friend he ever had, indeed his best friend, but now in his old age he thinks he never succeeded. The march-past commences. As they draw level with the first marker the commander gives the order "Eyes right!" Klein salutes the prince. Then, at the second marker, comes the order "Eyes front!" Emil drops out of the line here, and as he walks over to the dais to join the old guard gathered around the prince, he keeps his eyes fixed on Klein marching on unperturbed, determined to go on until the very end. Klein will march on no matter what, oblivious to those picking up the pieces, they can put him in a coffin and yet he will march on, they can shovel earth on the lid and yet Klein will march on, not for sentimental reasons, no, but because he is driven by an unconscionable faith in progress, a faith he was born with and which never left him. Emil feels a twinge in his chest. His head begins to reel. He curses Klein for failing to take notice the way he does. Klein could have known he had betrayed him; they would have been able to share his lies, and that would have meant being relieved of at least half the burden.

ACKNOWLEDGMENTS

Extracts of *Love's Death* first appeared in *De Revisor* 1996, no. 3/4, and in *Nieuw Wereldtijdschrift*, June 1998, no. 1. The image with which the novel opens (the sailor swallowing the end of a rope) derives from "The Schooner Banbury" by Witold Gombrowicz. Daisy echoes *The Catcher in the Rye* by J. D. Salinger in her personal notes. The book *Levenstijdperken van de man* (The Life Cycle of the Human Male), cited by Paul Klein, was written by Prof. dr. H. C. Rümke. Paul's letter to his father is based on the diary of Jac. Sinke, published in the commemorative book *Met 3-3 R.I. in de tropen* (1949). Details on paratrooper training are from *Korps Commandotroepen 1942–1982*, issued by the Commando Stichting. My father kindly allowed me to use his "motor log-book." Thanks are also due to Jan Kerkhof for brainstorming about the title.

JAN 1 0 2002